the secret
of evil

Also by Roberto Bolaño

AVAILABLE FROM NEW DIRECTIONS

Amulet

Antwerp

Between Parentheses

By Night in Chile

Distant Star

The Insufferable Gaucho

Last Evenings on Earth

Monsieur Pain

Nazi Literature in the Americas

The Return

The Romantic Dogs

The Skating Rink

Tres

Roberto Bolaño

the secret
of evil

Translated by CHRIS ANDREWS
with NATASHA WIMMER

 A NEW DIRECTIONS BOOK

Grateful acknowledgment is made to the magazines where some of these pieces originally appeared: *Granta*, *Harpers*, and *The New Yorker*.

PUBLISHER'S NOTE: Three pieces, "Vagaries of the Literature of Doom," "Beach," and "Sevilla Kills Me," appeared in Roberto Bolaño's *Between Parentheses* (New Directions, 2011), and are included here in Natasha Wimmer's translations. These pieces appeared in the original Spanish editions of both *El secreto del mal* and *Entre parentesis*.

Manufactured in the United States of America
Published simultaneously in Canada by Penguin Books Canada, Ltd.
New Directions Books are printed on acid-free paper.
First published as a New Directions Book in 2012

Library of Congress Cataloging-in-Publication Data
Bolaño, Roberto, 1953–2003.
[Secreto del mal. English]
The secret of evil / Roberto Bolaño ; translated by Chris Andrews and Natasha Wimmer.
— 1st American cloth ed.
p. cm.
"Originally published as El secreto del mal by Editorial Anagrama, Barcelona, Spain"—T.p. verso.
"A New Directions Book."
Texts Bolano was working on before he died: completed stories, sketches for larger works, essays, and fragments.
ISBN 978-0-8112-1815-3 (hardcover : alk. paper)
1. Bolaño, Roberto, 1953–2003—Translations into English. I. Andrews, Chris, 1962– II. Wimmer, Natasha. III. Title.
PQ8098.12.O38S4313 2012
863'.64—dc23
                              2011048681

10 9 8 7 6 5 4 3 2 1

New Directions Books are published for James Laughlin
by New Directions Publishing Corporation
80 Eighth Avenue, New York 10011
ndbooks.com

Contents

PRELIMINARY NOTE

This volume gathers a handful of stories and narrative sketches gleaned from the more than fifty files found on Roberto Bolaño's computer after his death. Many of those files contain poems, stories, novels, articles, talks and interviews that Bolaño had published during his lifetime or had prepared for publication. Other files contain poems and narrative sketches or fragments in various states of completion, sometimes on their own, but more often grouped and inventoried in what appear to be drafts of books, to which Bolaño himself, from a very early stage, would usually give a provisional title, and sometimes even a dedication. Such is the case with the file entitled "BAIRES," which has served as the basis for the composition of this volume. There are multiple indications that Bolaño was working on this file in the months immediately preceding his death, although there is no record of the dates on which the various files were created or modified. The conviction that this was one of the last documents on which Bolaño worked motivated the editors' decision to preserve the dedication that figured at the beginning of the file, after the title *New Stories*. The possibility of keeping that title was also considered, but in the end we chose to borrow the title of one of the stories in the file, which opens with a declaration that is apposite to many of the pieces collected here: "This story is very simple, although it could have been very complicated. Also, it's incomplete, because stories like this don't have an ending."

Bolaño's work as a whole remains suspended over the abysses that it dares to sound. All his narratives, not just *The Secret of Evil*, seem to be governed by a poetics of inconclusiveness. The eruption of horror seems to determine the interruption of the storytelling; or perhaps it is the other way around: the interruption of the telling suggests the imminence of horror. In any case, the inconclusive nature of Bolaño's novels and stories makes it difficult to decide which of the unpublished narrative texts should be regarded as finished and which are simply sketches. The task is further complicated by Bolaño's progressive radicalization of what I have called his poetics of inconclusiveness. And to make the distinction more difficult still, Bolaño rarely began to write a story without giving it a title and immediately establishing a definite tone and atmosphere; his writing, which is always captivating, virtually never stumbles or hesitates. Kafka's notebooks and posthumous papers place the reader in a similar situation: one is continually coming across marvelous narrative openings, which then break off abruptly. Decisions as to the wholeness and self-sufficiency of particular pieces can only be based on judgments that, although grounded, are inevitably subjective, and little would be gained by explaining them here.

Almost half the pieces in this volume come from the file mentioned above, specifically: "The Troublemaker," "The

Tour," "The Room Next Door," "Vagaries of the Literature of Doom," "The Colonel's Son," "Scholars of Sodom," "The Secret of Evil," and "Sevilla Kills Me" (in that order in the file). There is evidence to suggest that some of these pieces are unfinished. But we thought it better to let the reader form his or her own opinion on that matter. "Vagaries of the Literature of Doom" and "Sevilla Kills Me" are the texts of two addresses given by Bolaño (the second is clearly unfinished) and have been published in the posthumous volume *Between Parentheses* (Barcelona: Anagrama, 2004; New York: New Directions, 2011), despite which they are reproduced here in order to respect and continue a marked tendency, in Bolaño's late collections, to include non-narrative pieces, with the obvious intention of enriching the genre of the short story by blurring its boundaries.

The remaining pieces in this volume—"I Can't Read," "Labyrinth," "Daniela," "Death of Ulises," "Suntan," "Colonia Lindavista," "Beach," "The Old Man of the Mountain," "The Days of Chaos" and "Crimes"—come from a file labeled STORIX. The text entitled "Beach," first published in the newspaper *El Mundo* on August 17, 2000, appeared in *Between Parentheses*, but is republished here in what we consider to be a more appropriate context. As to "I Can't Read," which is clearly unfinished, its content is wholly autobiographical and the narrator is, without doubt, Roberto Bolaño himself; nevertheless, he refers to the text, in the first line, as "a story"—a clear indication of his increasingly open idea of the genre.

The piece entitled "Scholars of Sodom," which is no doubt incomplete, comes from a file labeled STOREC, and is in fact composed of two texts with the same title, the second, written some years later, taking the first as its starting point. In this volume, the two versions are given one after another, so as to form a sequence. Incidentally, Bolaño toyed with the idea of using the title "Scholars of Sodom" for a collection of stories very similar to the one that was finally published as *Murdering Whores* (*Putas asesinas*, Barcelona, Anagrama, 2001).

The long story entitled "Muscles," probably the beginning of an unfinished novel, perhaps an early version of *Una novelita lumpen* (Barcelona, Mondadori, 2002), is the only text in a file labeled MUSCLE.

All the texts are reproduced here without any changes apart from the correction of occasional oversights or literal errors. It is worth emphasizing that Bolaño's texts, whether written by hand or on a word processor, almost always exhibit a high degree of clarity and orderliness. As a result, the author's verbal intentions are unequivocal, and there has been no need for editorial reconstructions, which are always open to dispute.

The order in which the texts are presented here is the product of intuition rather than capricious decisions on the part of the editors, who hope not to have presumed too far or erred too much in their desire to endow the whole with a deliberate rhythm and an inner coherence.

IGNACIO ECHEVARRÍA
Barcelona, September 2005

for my children Lautaro and Alexandra

THE SECRET OF EVIL

COLONIA LINDAVISTA

When we arrived in Mexico, in 1968, a friend of my mother's put us up for the first few days, after which we rented an apartment in Colonia Lindavista. I've forgotten the name of the street; sometimes I think it was called Aurora, but maybe I'm getting mixed up. In Blanes I lived for a few years in an apartment on a Calle Aurora, so it seems unlikely that I lived on another Calle Aurora in Mexico, although the name's not all that unusual: quite a few cities have a street with that name. The Calle Aurora in Blanes, by the way, is no more than twenty yards long, and more like an alley than a street. The one in Colonia Lindavista, if it really was called Calle Aurora, was narrow but long, four blocks at least, and we lived there for the first year of our long residence in Mexico.

The woman we rented the apartment from was called Eulalia Martínez. She was a widow and she had three daughters and a son. She lived on the first floor of the building, a building that seemed normal to me at the time, but thinking back now, I see it as a conglomerate of oddities and blunders, because the second floor, which you got to by climbing an outdoor staircase, and the third floor, to which there was a metal ladder, had been added much later on and possibly without permits. The differences were striking: the apartment on the first floor had high ceilings and a certain dignity; it was ugly but it had been built according to an architect's plans. The second and third floors were the fruit of ad hoc interactions between Doña Eulalia's aesthetic sense and the skills of a builder friend. The reasoning behind this architectonic corpulence was not entirely mercenary. The owner of our apartment had four children, and the four apartments on the two additional floors had been built for them, so that they would stay close to their mother when they got married.

When we arrived, however, the only apartment that was occupied was the one directly above ours. Doña Eulalia's three daughters were unmarried and lived with their mother downstairs. The son, Pepe, who was the youngest, was the only one who had married, and he lived above us with his wife, Lupita. They were our closest neighbors during that time.

There's not much more I can say about Doña Eulalia. She was a strong-willed woman who'd been lucky in life, and she may not have been a very nice person. I scarcely knew her daughters. They were what used to be known, in those long-gone years, as old maids, and they endured their fate with all the grace they could muster, which is to say not very much; at best they gave off a dingy kind of resignation, which stained the things around them or the way I remember those things now that they've all disappeared. The daughters were rarely to be seen, or at least I didn't see them much; they watched soap operas and gossiped spitefully about the other women in the neighborhood, whom they saw at the grocer's or in the dark entrance way where a skeletal Indian woman sold *nixtamal* tortillas.

Pepe and his wife, Lupita, were different.

My mother and father, who were three or four years younger than I am now, made friends with them almost right away. I was interested in Pepe. In the neighborhood all the boys my age called him "The Pilot" because he flew for the Mexican Air Force. Lupita was a housewife. Before getting married she had worked as a secretary or a clerk in a government office. Both of them were friendly and hospitable, or tried to be. Sometimes my parents would go up to their apartment and stay there a while, listening to records and drinking. My parents were older than Pepe and Lupita, but they were Chilean, and at the time Chileans saw themselves as the acme of modernity, at least in Latin America. The age gap was offset by the markedly youthful spirit of my progenitors.

On a few occasions I went up to their apartment too. The living room (which we called a *living*) was relatively modern, and Pepe had a record player that seemed to be a recent acquisition. On the walls and the sideboards in the dining room there were photos of him and Lupita, and photos of the airplanes he flew, which were what interested me the most; but he preferred not to talk about his work, as if he were always protecting some military secret. Classified information, as they said in the North American TV shows. The secrets of the Mexican Air Force, which, frankly, no one was losing any sleep over, except for Pepe with his somewhat extravagant sense of duty and responsibility.

Little by little, from conversations at the dinner table or overheard while I was studying, I began to get a sense of what our neighbors' life was really like. They'd been married for five years and still didn't have any children. There were frequent visits to the gynecologist. According to the doctors, Lupita was perfectly capable of having children. And the tests showed that Pepe was the same. The problem was mental, the doctors said. As the years went by, Pepe's mother began to resent the fact that Lupita hadn't provided her with grandchildren. Lupita once confessed to my mother that the problem was the apartment, and being so close to her mother-in-law. If they went somewhere else, she said, she'd probably be able to get pregnant right away.

I think Lupita was right.

Another thing: Pepe and Lupita were short. I was taller than Pepe and I was seventeen at the time. So I guess Pepe can't have been more than five foot nine, and Lupita would have been about five foot two at the most. Pepe was dark, with very black hair, and a thoughtful expression, as if there was always something on his mind. Every morning he went to work wearing his air force officer's uniform. He was always impeccably turned out, except on the weekend, when he put on a sweatshirt and jeans and didn't shave. Lupita had fair skin, dyed-blonde hair, and a more or less permanent perm, which she used to get done at the hairdresser's, or did herself, using a little kit containing all a woman's hair needs, which Pepe brought back from the United States. She used to smile when she said hello. Sometimes from my room I could hear them having sex. This was around the time I started getting serious about writing and I used to stay up very late. My life seemed pretty dull to me. In fact I was dissatisfied with everything about it. I used to write until two or three in the morning, and that was when the groans would suddenly begin in the apartment upstairs.

At first it all seemed normal. If Pepe and Lupita wanted to have a child they had to fuck. But then I asked myself, Why were they starting so late at night? Why couldn't I hear any voices *before* the groans began? Needless to say, my knowledge of sex at the time was limited to what I'd been able to glean from movies and porn magazines. In other words, it was minimal. But I knew enough to sense that something strange was happening in the apartment upstairs. In my imagination, I began to embellish Pepe and Lupita's sex life with incomprehensible gestures, as if sadomasochistic scenes were being played out upstairs, scenes that I couldn't completely visualize, that weren't built around actions intended to produce pain or pleasure, but around dramatized movements that Pepe and Lupita were executing in spite of themselves, movements that were gradually unhinging them.

None of this was obvious from the outside. And in fact I soon reached the smug conclusion that nobody else had noticed. My mother, who was, in a way, Lupita's friend and confidante, thought that all the couple's problems would be solved by moving away. My father had no opinion on the matter. Freshly arrived in Mexico, we were too busy taking in all the new things that dazzled us every day to puzzle over the secret life of our neighbors. When I think back to that time, I see my parents and my sister, and then I see myself, and the little group we compose looks overwhelmingly desolate.

Six blocks from our house there was a Gigante supermarket where we went on Saturdays to shop for the whole week. That's something I can remember in elaborate detail. I also remember that I was sent to an Opus Dei high school, although in defense of my parents I should point out that they had never heard of Opus Dei. It took me more than a year myself to realize what a diabolical place it was. My Ethics teacher was a self-confessed Nazi, which was weird, because he was a little guy from Chiapas with indigenous features, who'd studied in Italy on a scholarship—a nice, dumb guy, basically, who would have been gassed by the real Nazis without a second thought—and my Logic teacher believed in the heroic will of José Antonio (many years later, in Spain, I ended up living on an avenue named after José Antonio). But, at the beginning, like my parents, I had no idea what was going on at that school.

Pepe and Lupita were the only people who interested me. And a friend of Pepe's, his only friend, actually, a fair-haired guy, the best pilot in his year at the academy, a tall thin guy who'd been injured in an accident when his fighter crashed and would never be able to fly again. He turned up at the house almost every weekend, and after saying hello to Pepe's mother and his sisters, who adored him, he went up to his friend's apartment and stayed there drinking and watching TV while Lupita made dinner. Sometimes he came during the week, and then he would be wearing his uniform, a uniform I have trouble visualizing now; I would have said it was blue, but I could be wrong, and if I shut my eyes and try to conjure up the image of Pepe and his fair-haired friend, I see them wearing green uniforms, light green, a dashing pair of pilots, alongside Lupita, who's wearing a white blouse and a blue skirt (she's the one wearing blue).

Sometimes the fair-haired guy stayed for dinner. My parents would go to bed while the music went on playing upstairs. I'd be the only one awake in our apartment, because that's when I used to start writing. And in a way the noise from the apartment upstairs kept me company. At about two in the morning, the voices and the music would stop and a strange silence would fill the whole building: not just Pepe's apartment but ours as well and the apartment where Pepe's mother lived, which was holding up the extensions and seemed to creak at that time of night, as if the weight of the extra stories was too much to bear. And then I could only hear the wind, the night wind of Mexico City, and the steps of the fair-haired guy as he walked to the door, accompanied by Pepe's steps, then the sound of footsteps on the stairs, and on our landing, and then going down the next flight of stairs to the ground floor, and the iron gate opening, and the steps fading away down Calle Aurora. Then I'd stop writing (I can't remember what I was writing, something awful, probably, but something long that kept me absorbed) and listen for the sounds that didn't come from Pepe's apartment, as if after the fair-haired guy had left, everything in there, including Pepe and Lupita, had suddenly frozen.

THE SECRET OF EVIL

This story is very simple, although it could have been very complicated. Also, it's incomplete, because stories like this don't have an ending. It's night in Paris, and a North American journalist is sleeping. Suddenly the telephone rings, and someone asks in English, with an unidentifiable accent, for Joe A. Kelso. Speaking, says the journalist and then looks at his watch. It's four in the morning; he's only had about three hours sleep and he's tired. The voice on the other end of the line says, I have to see you, to pass on some information. The journalist asks him what it's about. As usual with calls like this, the voice gives nothing away. The journalist asks for some indication, at least. In impeccable English, far more correct than Kelso's, the voice expresses a preference for a face-to-face meeting. Then, straight away, it adds, There is no time to lose. Where? Kelso asks. The voice mentions one of the bridges over the Seine. And adds: You can get there in twenty minutes on foot. The journalist, who has had hundreds of meetings like this, says that he'll be there in half an hour. Getting dressed, he thinks it's a pretty stupid way to waste the night, and yet he realizes, with a slight shock of surprise, that he's no longer sleepy, that the call, in spite of its predictability, has left him wide awake. When he reaches the bridge, five minutes after the appointed time, he can see nothing but cars. For a while he stands still at one end, waiting. Then he walks across the bridge, which is still deserted, and after waiting for a few minutes at the other end, finally crosses back again and decides to give up and go home to bed. While he's walking home, he thinks about the voice: it definitely wasn't a North American voice and it probably wasn't British either, though he's not so sure about that now. It could have been a South African or an Australian, he thinks, or a Dutchman, maybe, or someone from northern Europe who learned English at school and has since perfected his command of the language in various Anglophone countries. As he crosses the street he hears someone call his name: Mr. Kelso. He realizes straight away that it's the man who arranged to meet him on the bridge, speaking from a dark entrance way. Kelso is about to stop, but the voice instructs him to keep walking. When he reaches the next corner, he turns around and sees that no one is following him. He's tempted to retrace his steps, but after a moment's hesitation he decides that it's best to continue on his way. Suddenly the man appears from a side street and greets him. Kelso returns his greeting. The man holds out his hand. Sacha Pinsky, he says. Kelso shakes his hand and introduces himself in turn. Pinsky pats him on the back and asks if he'd like a whiskey. A little whiskey, is what he actually says. He asks Kelso if he's hungry. He assures the journalist that he knows a bar where they can get hot croissants, freshly baked. Kelso looks at his face. Although Pinsky is wearing a hat, his face is a pasty white, as if he'd been locked away for years and years. But where? Kelso wonders. In a prison or an institution for the mentally ill. In any case, it's too late to pull out now, and Kelso wouldn't mind a hot croissant. The place is called Chez Pain, and in spite of the fact that it's in his neighborhood (in a narrow side street, admittedly), this is the first time he's set foot inside, and perhaps the first time he's even seen it. Mostly he frequents establishments in Montparnasse with a dubious air of legend about them: the place where Scott Fitzgerald once ate, the place where Joyce and Beckett drank Irish whiskey, the bars favored by Hemingway and Dos Passos, Truman Capote and Tennessee Williams. Pinsky was right about the croissants at Chez Pain: they're good, they're freshly baked, and the coffee isn't bad at all. Which makes Kelso think—and it's a chilling thought—that this guy could well be a local, a neighbor. As he considers this possibility, Kelso is seized by a shudder. A bore, a paranoiac, a madman, a watcher with no one to watch him in turn, someone it's going be hard to get rid of. Well, he eventually says, I'm listening. The pale man, who is sipping his coffee but not eating, looks at him and smiles. There is something intensely sad about his smile, and tired as well, as if it were the only way in which he could allow himself to express his tiredness, his exhaustion and lack of sleep. But as soon as he stops smiling, his features recover their iciness.

THE OLD MAN OF THE MOUNTAIN

Things are always happening by chance. One day Belano meets Lima, and they become friends. Both live in Mexico City and their friendship, like those of many young poets, is sealed by a common rejection of certain social norms and by the literary affinities they share. As I said, they're young. They're very young, in fact, and full of energy, in their own way, and they believe in literature's analgesic powers. They recite Homer and Frank O'Hara, Archilocus and John Giorno, and although they don't know it, their lives are running along the brink of the abyss.

One day—this is in 1975—Belano says that William Burroughs is dead, and when Lima hears the news he goes very pale and says, He can't be, Burroughs is alive. Belano doesn't insist; he says he thinks that Burroughs is dead, but maybe he's mistaken. When did he die? asks Lima. Not long ago, I think, says Belano, feeling less and less sure, I read it somewhere.

What intervenes at this point in the story is something that might be called a silence. Or a gap. A very short gap, in any case, and yet, for Belano, it opens up and will last, mysteriously, until the century's final years.

Two days later, Lima turns up with proof, and it's indisputable, that Burroughs is alive.

Years go by. Occasionally, just occasionally, and without knowing why, Belano remembers the day on which he arbitrarily announced the death of Burroughs. It was a clear day; he was walking with Lima on Calle Sullivan; they'd left a friend's place and the rest of the day was free. They might have been talking about the Beats. Then he said that Burroughs was dead, and Lima went pale and said, He can't be. Sometimes Belano thinks he can remember Lima shouting: He can't be! It's impossible. Unjust. Or something like that. He also remembers Lima's grief, as if he'd been told of the death of a very dear relative, a grief (although Belano knows that *grief* is not the right word) that persisted through the following days, until Lima was able to confirm that the information was incorrect. Something about that day, however, something indefinable, leaves a trace of uneasiness in Belano. Uneasiness and joy. The uneasiness is actually fear in disguise. And the joy? Belano generally thinks, or wants to believe, that what lies hidden behind the joy is nostalgia for his own youth, but what lies hidden is really ferocity: a dark, enclosed space busy with blurry figures, adhering to one another or superimposed, and constantly on the move. Figures that feed on a violence they can barely control (or can only control by means of a very strange economy). Although it seems counterintuitive, there is an airy quality to the uneasiness provoked by the memory of that day. And the joy is subterranean, like a geometric ship, perfectly rectangular in shape, gliding along a groove.

Sometimes Belano examines the groove.

He leans forward, he bends over, his spinal column curves like the trunk of a tree in a storm and he examines the groove: a deep, clean trace, parting a strange kind of skin, the mere sight of which makes him feel nauseous. The years go by. And they rewind. In 1975 Belano and Lima are friends, and every day they walk, unknowingly, along the brink of the abyss. Until one day they leave Mexico. Lima sets off for France and Belano for Spain. From now on, their lives, which have been joined, will follow different paths. Lima travels through Europe and the Middle East. Belano travels through Europe and Africa. Both fall in love, both try in vain to find happiness or to get themselves killed. Eventually, years later, Belano settles down in a village by the Mediterranean. Lima returns to Mexico. He returns to Mexico City.

But things have happened in the meantime. In 1975, Mexico City is a radiant place. Belano and Lima publish their poems, usually together, in the same magazines, and participate in readings at the Casa del Lago. By 1976, both are known to, and above all feared by, a literary establishment that simply cannot stand them. Two wild, suicidal ants. Belano and Lima lead a group of adolescent poets who have no respect for anyone. Anyone at all. An unforgivable offence for the literary powers that be; Belano and Lima are blackballed. This is in 1976. At the end of the year, Lima, who is Mexican, leaves the country. Shortly afterward, in January 1977, Belano, who is Chilean, follows him.

That's how it goes. 1975. 1976. Two young men sentenced to life. Europe. A new phase beginning and—as it begins— pulling them back from the brink of the abyss. And separation, because although it's true that Belano and Lima meet in Paris and then in Barcelona and then in a railway station in Rousillon, their destinies eventually diverge and their bodies move apart, like two arrows suddenly, inevitably, veering off on separate trajectories.

So that's how it goes. 1977. 1978. 1979. And then 1980, and the '80s, a black decade for Latin America.

All the same, every now and then, Belano and Lima hear news of each other. Belano, especially, hears about Lima. One day, for instance, he hears that his old friend has been hit by a bus, and miraculously survived. The accident leaves Lima with a limp for the rest of his life. It also converts him into a legend. Or that's what Belano thinks, anyway, far away from Mexico City. From time to time, a friend who lives in Barcelona has visitors from Mexico, who bring news of Lima, which the friend then passes on to Belano.

THE COLONEL'S SON

You're not going to believe this, but last night, at about four a.m., I saw a movie on TV that could have been my biography or my autobiography or a summary of my days on this bitch of a planet. It scared me so fucking shitless I tell you I just about fell off my chair.

I was stunned. I could tell right away the film was bad, or the sort we call bad—poor fools that we are—because the actors aren't much good and the director's not much good and the cretinous special effects guys are pretty hopeless too. But really it was just a very low-budget film, pure B-grade schlock. What I mean, just to be perfectly clear, is a film that cost about four euros or five dollars. I don't know who they conned to raise the money, but I can tell you that all the producer shelled out was a bit of small change, and they had to make do with that.

I can't even remember the title, really I can't, but I'll go to my grave calling it *The Colonel's Son*, and I swear it was the most democratic, the most revolutionary film I'd seen in ages, and I don't say that because the film in itself revolutionized anything, not at all, it was pathetic really, full of clichés and tired devices, prejudice and stereotypes, and yet at the same time every frame was infused with and gave off a revolutionary atmosphere, or rather an atmosphere in which you could sense the revolution, not in its totality, but a fragment, a minuscule, microscopic fragment of the revolution, as if you were watching *Jurassic Park*, say, except the dinosaurs never showed, no, I mean as if it was *Jurassic Park* and no one ever even *mentioned* the fucking reptiles, but their presence was inescapable and unbearably oppressive.

Do you see what I getting at? I've never read any of Osvaldo Lamborghini's *Proletarian Chamber Theater*, but I'm certain that Lamborghini, with his masochistic streak, would have been happy to watch *The Colonel's Son* at three or four in the morning. What was it about? Well, don't laugh, it was about zombies. No kidding, like George Romero's movies, more or less; it had to be a kind of homage to Romero's two great zombie flicks. But if the political background to Romero is Karl Marx, the political background to the movie last night was Arthur Rimbaud and Alfred Jarry. Pure French insanity.

Don't laugh. Romero is straightforward and tragic: he talks about communities sinking into the mire and about survivors. He also has a sense of humor. You remember his second film, the one where the zombies wander around the mall because that's the only place they can vaguely remember from their previous lives? Well, last night's film was different. It didn't have much of a sense of humor, although I laughed like a madman, and it wasn't about a communal tragedy either. The protagonist was a boy who—I'm guessing, because I didn't see the start—turns up one day with his girlfriend at the place where his father works. I didn't see the start, like I said, so I can't be sure. Maybe the boy goes to visit his father and that's where he meets the girl. Her name is Julie and she's pretty and young, and she wants to be—or seem to be—up to date, the way young people do. The boy is the son of Colonel Reynolds. The colonel is a widower and loves his son—that's obvious right from the start—but he's also a soldier, so the relationship that he has with his son is one in which there's no place for displays of affection.

What is Julie doing at the base? We don't know. Maybe she went to deliver some pizzas and got lost. Maybe she's the sister of one of the guinea pigs that Colonel Reynolds is using, although that seems unlikely. Maybe she met the colonel's son when she was hitching a ride out of the city. What we do know is that Julie is there and that at some point she gets lost in an underground labyrinth and innocently walks through a door that she never should have opened. On the other side is a zombie, and it starts chasing her. Julie flees, of course, but the zombie manages to corner her and scratch her; at one point he even bites her arm and her legs. The scene is suggestive of a rape. Then the colonel's son, who's been searching for her, appears, and between them they manage to overpower and kill the zombie, if such a thing is possible. Then they flee down increasingly narrow and tortuous underground passages, until they finally make their way out through the sewers to the surface. As they're escaping, Julie begins to feel the first symptoms of the illness. She's tired and hungry and begs the colonel's son to leave her or forget her. His resolve, however, is unshakeable. He has fallen in love with Julie, or perhaps he was already in love (which suggests that he has known her for some time); in any case, armed with the generosity of the very young, he has no intention, come what may, of leaving her to face her fate alone.

When they reach the surface, Julie's hunger is uncontrollable. The streets have a desolate look. The film was probably shot on the outskirts of some North American city: deserted neighborhoods, the sort of half-derelict buildings that directors who have no budget use for shooting after midnight. That's where they end up, the colonel's son and Julie, who's hungry; she's been complaining all the time they were running away. It hurts, I'm hungry: but the colonel's son doesn't seem to hear; all he cares about is saving her, getting away from the military base, and never seeing his father again.

The relationship between father and son is odd. It's clear from the start that the colonel puts his son before his duties as a soldier, but of course his love isn't reciprocated; the son has a long way to go before he'll be able to understand his father, or solitude, or the sad fate to which all beings are condemned. Young Reynolds is, after all, an adolescent, and he's in love and nothing else matters to him. But careful, don't be misled by appearances. The son appears to be a young fool, a young hothead, rash and thoughtless, just like we were, except that he speaks English, and his particular desert is a devastated neighborhood in a North American megalopolis, while we spoke Spanish (of a kind) and lived, stifled, on desolate avenues in the cities of Latin America.

When the two of them emerge from the maze of underground passages, the landscape is somehow familiar to us. The lighting is poor; the windows of the buildings are smashed; there are hardly any cars on the streets.

The colonel's son drags Julie to a food store. One of those stores that stays open till three or four in the morning. A filthy store where tins of food are stacked up next to chocolate bars and bags of potato chips. There's only one guy working there. Naturally, he's an immigrant, and to judge from his age and the look of anxiety and annoyance that comes over his face, he must be the owner. The colonel's son leads Julie to the counter where the donuts and the sweets are, but Julie goes straight to the fridge and starts eating a raw hamburger. The storekeeper is watching them through the one-way mirror, and when he sees her throw up he comes out and asks if they're trying to eat without paying. The colonel's son reaches into the pocket of his jeans and throws him some bills.

At this point four people come in. They're Mexicans. It's not hard to imagine them taking classes at a drama school, or, for that matter, dealing drugs on the corners of their neighborhood, or picking tomatoes with John Steinbeck's farmhands. Three guys and a girl, in their twenties, mindless and prepared to die in any old alleyway. The Mexicans show an interest in Julie's vomit too. The storekeeper says the money's not enough. The colonel's son says it is. Who's going to pay for the damage? Who's going to pay for this filth? says the storekeeper, pointing at the vomit, which is a nuclear shade of green. While they're arguing, one of the Mexicans has slipped in behind the till and is emptying it. Meanwhile the other three are staring at the vomit as if it concealed the secret of the universe.

When the storekeeper realizes he's being robbed, he pulls out a pistol and threatens the Mexicans. This gives the colonel's son a chance to grab a few sweets from the counter and beg Julie to get out of there with him, but Julie has gone back to the raw meat, and as she tears into a steak, she begins to cry and says she doesn't understand and implores young Reynolds to do something. The Mexicans start brawling with the storekeeper. They pull out their knives and flash them in the bluish light of the food store. They manage to get hold of the storekeeper's pistol and shoot him. He drops to the floor. One of the Mexicans goes to the counter where the alcoholic drinks are kept and grabs some bottles without bothering to see what kind of liquor they contain. As he passes Julie, she bites him on the arm. The Mexican howls. Julie sinks her teeth in and won't let go, despite the pleas of the colonel's son. Another gunshot.

Someone shouts, C'mon, let's go. The Mexican manages to pull his arm free and catches up with his companions, crying out in pain. Young Reynolds examines the storekeeper's body lying on the floor. He's alive, he says, we have to get him to a hospital. No, says Julie, leave him, the police will take care of him. Their steps, as they walk out of the store, are quick but unsteady. They see a black van parked outside and break into it. Just as young Reynolds manages to get it going, the store-keeper appears and begs them to take him to a hospital. Julie looks at him but doesn't say a word. The storekeeper's white shirt is stained with blood. The colonel's son tells him to get in. When he's in the van and they're about to go, they hear the siren of a police car. Then the storekeeper says he wants to get out. Can't do that, says the colonel's son, and tears away.

The chase begins. It doesn't take long for the police to start shooting. The storekeeper opens the van's back door and shouts, That's enough. He's cut down by a hail of bullets. Julie, who's sitting in the back seat, turns and peers into the darkness. She hears him crying. The storekeeper is crying for the life that's slipping away from him, a life of ceaseless work and struggling in a foreign land to give his family a better future. And now it's all over.

Then Julie gets out of her seat and goes into the back part of the van. And while the colonel's son shakes off the police, Julie starts eating the storekeeper's chest. With a radiant smile on his face, young Reynolds turns to Julie and says, We've lost the cops, but she is crouched on all fours in the back, as if she were a tiger or were making love, and her only reaction is to breathe a satisfied sigh, because she's assuaged her appetite; momentarily, as we shall soon discover. All the colonel's son can do, of course, is cry out in terror. Then he says: What've you done, Julie? How could you do that? It's clear from his tone of voice, however, that he's in love, and that although his girl's a cannibal, she is, in spite of everything, his girl. Julie's reply is simple: she was hungry.

At this point, while young Reynolds is mutely venting his exasperation, the police car appears again and the young pair resume their flight through dark, deserted streets. There's still a surprise in store for us: when the police open fire on the fugitives, the back door of the van opens, and the storekeeper appears, but he's become a ravenous zombie. First he tears open a cop's throat, then sets on the guy's partner, who empties the magazine of his gun at him, in vain, then freezes in horror, before being devoured in turn. Just then two cars from the military base close off the alley, and using two rather strange weapons, like laser guns, neutralize first the storekeeper and then the two zombie policemen. Colonel Reynolds gets out of one of the cars and asks his soldiers if they've seen his son. The soldiers reply in the negative. Another car appears in the alley and a woman, Colonel Landovski, gets out. She informs Reynolds that from now on, she'll be in charge of the operation. Reynolds says he doesn't give a damn who's in charge, all he wants is to find his son safe and sound. Your son's probably been infected by now, says Colonel Landovski. It's an odd scene: Landovski takes on the role of "father," prepared to sacrifice the boy, while Reynolds takes on the role of "mother," prepared to do anything to ensure the survival of his son. A fifth or sixth car pulls up at the corner, but no one gets out. It's the Mexicans.

They recognize the van from the food store, the van in which the young lovers fled. One of the Mexicans, the one Julie bit, is pretty sick. He's running a fever and raving incoherently. He wants to eat. I'm hungry, he keeps telling his friends. He asks them to take him to a hospital. The Mexican girl backs him up. We have to take him to a hospital, she says sensibly. The other two agree, but first they want to find the bitch who bit Chucho and teach her a lesson she'll never forget.

Since we forget everything in the end, I'm only guessing that they talk about killing her. They're spurring each other on to vengeance. They speak of honor, respect, principles, the right thing. Then they start the car and drive off. At no point do the soldiers show any sign of having noticed them, as if this ghostly street were a busy thoroughfare.

In the following scene Julie and young Reynolds are walking over a bridge. Where can we find a taxi? the boy wonders. Julie announces that she can't walk any further. On the other side of the bridge is a phone booth. Wait for me here, says young Reynolds, and runs off toward the booth, only to find that there's no phonebook and that the receiver has been ripped out. Looking back, he sees that Julie has climbed onto the balustrade of the bridge. He shouts, Julie, don't! and starts running. But Julie jumps and her body disappears into the water, although it soon floats to the surface and is swept away by the current, face down. The colonel's son goes down a stairway to the river. The water is very shallow: a foot, three feet at the deepest. The river has man-made banks and even the bed has been paved. A homeless black man, hidden among some concrete pillars down the river, is watching young Reynolds. The boy's search brings him near this man, who tells him to give up, the girl is dead. No, says the colonel's son, no, and goes on searching, closely followed by the black guy.

When young Reynolds finds her, the girl is floating in a pool. Julie, Julie, calls her young lover, and the girl, who has been face down in the water for who knows how many minutes, coughs and calls his name. All my fucking life I've never seen anything like that, says the black guy.

Just then, the Mexicans appear (the verb *to appear* will appear often in this story), fifty yards away. They've gotten out of their car and are looking on; one is sitting on the hood, another leaning against a fender, and the girl is up on the roof; only the wounded guy is still inside, watching or trying to watch them through the window. The Mexicans make menacing gestures and threaten them with a litany of punishments, tortures and humiliations. This is getting nasty, says the black guy. Follow me. They enter the city's system of sewers. The Mexicans follow them. But the labyrinth of tunnels is sufficiently complicated for the black guy and the young couple to lose their pursuers. Finally they reach a refuge that's almost as welcoming as a nightclub. This is my place, says the black guy. Then he tells them the story of his life. The jobs he's had to do. The constant presence of the police. The hardbitten life of a North American working man in the twentieth or twenty-first century. My muscles couldn't take any more, says the black guy.

His place isn't bad. He has a bed, where they lay Julie down, and books, which, so he says, he's picked up over the years in the sewers. Self-help books and books about the revolution and books on technical subjects, like how to repair a lawn mower. There's also a kind of bathroom, with a primitive shower. This water's always clean, says the black guy. A stream of crystal-clear water falls continually from a hole in the ceiling. We all build our places with whatever we can find, he explains. Then he picks up an iron bar and says that they can rest; he'll go out and keep watch.

It's always night in the sewers, but that night, the last night of peace, is particularly strange. The boy falls asleep in a shabby armchair after making love with Julie. The black guy falls asleep too, mumbling incomprehensibly. The girl is the only one who doesn't feel sleepy, and she goes into other rooms, because her appetite has begun to rage again. But with a difference: now Julie knows that self-inflicted pain can be a substitute for food. So we see her sticking needles in her face and piercing her nipples with wires.

At this point the Mexicans reappear and easily overpower

first the black guy, then the son of Colonel Reynolds. They look for the girl. They shout threats. If she doesn't come out of her hiding place, they'll kill the black guy and her boyfriend. Then a door opens and Julie appears. She has changed a lot. She has become the indisputable queen of piercing. The leader of the Mexicans (the biggest guy) finds her attractive. The sick Mexican is lying on the ground, begging them to take him to a hospital. The Mexican girl is comforting him, but her eyes are fixed on the new Julie. The other Mexican is holding the colonel's son, who is screaming like a man possessed; the possibility (or the strong probability) that Julie will be raped is more than he can bear. The black guy is lying unconscious on the ground.

Julie and the Mexican go into in a room and shut the door. No, Julie, no, no, no, sobs young Reynolds. The Mexican's voice can be heard through the door: That's it, baby. C'mon, let's get that off. Holy shit! You really do like those hooks, don't you? Kneel down baby, yeah, that's it, that's it. Lift up your ass, perfect, oh yeah. And more stuff like that until suddenly he starts yelling, and there are blows, as if someone was getting kicked, or thrown against a wall, then picked up and thrown against the opposite wall, and then the yelling stops and there's only the sound of biting and chewing, until the door opens and Julie appears again with her lips (and in fact the whole of her face) smeared with blood, holding the Mexican's head in one hand.

Which makes the other Mexican go crazy; he pulls out a pistol, goes up to Julie and empties it into her, but of course the bullets don't harm her at all, and she laughs contentedly before grabbing the guy's shirt, pulling him toward her and tearing his throat open with a single bite. Young Reynolds and the black guy, who has recovered consciousness, are gaping at the scene. The Mexican girl, however, has the presence of mind to try to escape, but Julie catches her as she's climbing a metal stairway that leads to the mouth of the upper sewer.

The girl kicks and curses furiously, but then, yielding to Julie's greater strength, she lets go and falls. Don't do it, Julie, the colonel's son has just enough time to say, before his sweetheart's teeth destroy the face of the Mexican girl. Then Julie extracts her victim's heart and eats it.

At this point, a voice says: So you think you've won, you whore. Julie turns around and what we see is the last Mexican, now fully transformed into a zombie. The two of them begin to fight. Julie is helped by the black guy and her boyfriend and for a few seconds it looks like she's going to win. But Julie's victims pick themselves up and join in the fight, and zombies, it seems, are ten times stronger than normal humans, which means that the fight inevitably begins to go the Mexicans' way. So our three heroes flee. The black guy takes them to a room. They barricade the door. The black guy tells them to go; he'll try, God knows how, to stop the zombies. Julie and young Reynolds don't have to be told twice, and go off to another room. At one point in their flight, Julie looks her boyfriend in the eye and asks him, just with her gaze or maybe with words, I can't remember now, how he can still love her. Young Reynolds replies by kissing her on the cheek, then he wipes his lips and kisses her on the mouth. I love you, he says, I love you more than ever.

Then they hear a yell and they know that the black guy is gone. There's no way out of the room where they've taken refuge; it's full of old furniture piled up chaotically, but with passages between; it's like a labyrinth of the transient, of things without the will to last. I have to leave you, says Julie. Young Reynolds doesn't know what she means. Only when Julie uses her extraordinary strength to throw him under some armchairs and broken-down washing machines and faulty or obsolete television sets does he understand that the girl is prepared to sacrifice herself for him. He hardly has time to react. Julie goes out and fights and loses and the Mexican zombies are coming for him. With tears streaming down his face, young Reynolds tries to make himself invisible, curling up into a ball of flesh under the pile of junk.

The Mexican zombies, however, find him and try to drag him out of there. Young Reynolds sees their hungry faces, then the hungry face of the black guy and Julie's face, watching him, showing no sign of emotion. At this point, Colonel Reynolds, escorted by three of his men, kicks down the door and starts blowing away all the zombies with the special gun. All the time he's firing, the colonel is calling his son's name. Here I am, Dad, says young Reynolds.

The nightmare is over.

The next scene shows the colonel comfortably seated in his office proposing to his son that they go to Alaska for a vacation together. Young Reynolds says he'll think it over. There's no rush, son, says the colonel. Then the colonel's on his own and he begins to smile to himself, as if he can't quite believe how incredibly lucky he's been. His son is alive. Meanwhile, young Reynolds has left his father's office and started walking through the underground passageways at the base. There's a look of deep uneasiness on his face. Gradually, however, distant noises begin to penetrate his self-absorption. He can hear shouts and howls, the cries of people for whom pain has become a way of life. Barely aware of what he's doing, he starts walking toward the source of the cries. He doesn't have to go far. The passage turns a corner and there is a door; it opens onto an enormous laboratory, stretching away before him.

He is warmly greeted by some military scientists who have known him since he was a boy. He continues on his way. He discovers a series of glass cells. The Mexicans have been placed in them, each in a separate cell. He keeps walking. He finds Julie's cell. Julie recognizes him. The colonel's son puts his hand on the glass and Julie puts her hand up to his, as if she were touching it. In a larger cell some scientists are working on the black guy. He could become a great warrior, they say. They are sending electric shocks through his brain. The black guy is full of hatred and resentment. He howls. The colonel's son hides in a corner. When the scientists go for their coffee break, he gets up and asks the black guy if he recognizes him. Vaguely, says the black guy. All my memories are vague. And fucking strange, too.

We were friends, says the colonel's son. We met by the river. I remember an apartment on 30th Street, says the black guy, and a woman laughing, but I don't know what I was doing there. The boy frees the black guy from his chains. Freed, he walks like a kind of robocop. A zombie robocop. Don't attack me, says the colonel's son, I'm your friend. I understand, says the black guy, who goes to a shelf and takes down an assault rifle. When the scientists come back, the black guy greets them with a volley of fire. Meanwhile the boy frees Julie and tells her that they have to flee again. They kiss. The soldiers try to take out the black guy. As Julie and her boyfriend are sneaking away, she frees the Mexicans. More soldiers arrive. The bullets destroy some containers where body parts are kept. Viscera and spinal columns crawl over the floor of the laboratory. A siren begins to shriek. In this pitched battle it isn't clear which side has the advantage, or even if there really are sides, not just individuals fighting for their own lives and for the deaths of the others. Over the PA a voice is repeating: Block the passages on level five. My son! shouts Colonel Reynolds and rushes down to level five like a madman.

Colonel Landovski shoots the black guy to bits and is de-voured in turn by the Mexican girl. The soldiers repel an at-tack mounted by bloody pieces of human flesh. The second attack, however, breaks through their lines of defense and they're devoured by tiny scraps of raw meat. There are more and more zombies. The battle becomes totally chaotic. The colonel reaches level five. Through a window he sees his son and Julie, and gestures to show that the passage is still open, there is still an escape route. The colonel's son takes Julie by the hand and they head in the direction that his father indicated. I'm hurting all over, says Julie. Don't start that again, says the boy, when we get away from here you'll feel better. Do you believe me? I believe you, says Julie.

In the passage that hasn't yet been blocked, Colonel Reynolds appears, unarmed, his shirt drenched with sweat, not only because he hasn't stopped running but also because the temperature on level five has increased dramatically. Colonel Reynolds' face has been transfigured. It could be said that his expression resembles that of Abraham. With every cell in his body he calls out his son's name and repeats how dearly he loves him. His military career, his scientific research, duty, honor and his country are all swept away by the force of love. Here, through here. Follow me. Hurry up. Soon the doors will shut automatically. Come with me and you'll be able to escape. All he gets in response is the sad gaze of his son, who at this moment, and perhaps for the first time, *knows* more than his father. The father at one end of the passage. The son at the other end. And suddenly the doors shut and they're separated forever.

Behind the son there's a kind of furnace. It isn't clear whether the furnace was there already or whether the fire caused by the zombie rebellion has spread. It's some blaze. Julie and the boy hold hands. Come on, Julie, says the boy, don't be afraid, nothing will separate us now. Meanwhile, on the other side, the colonel is trying to break down the door, in vain. His son and Julie walk toward the fire. On the other side, the colonel beats at the door with his fists. His knuckles go red with blood. I'm not afraid, says Julie. I love you, says young Reynolds. On the other side, the colonel is trying to break down the door, in vain. The young lovers walk toward the fire and disappear. The screen goes an intense red. The only sound is a machine gun hammering. Then an explosion, screams, groans, electrical sparking. On the other side, shut off from all this, the colonel is trying to break down the door, in vain.

SCHOLARS OF SODOM

for Celina Manzoni

I.

It's 1972 and I can see V. S. Naipaul strolling through the streets of Buenos Aires. Well, sometimes he's strolling, but sometimes, when he's on his way to meetings or keeping appointments, his gait is quick and his eyes take in only what he needs to see in order to reach his destination with a minimum of bother, whether it's a private dwelling or, more often, a restaurant or a café, since many of those who've agreed to meet him have chosen a public place, as if they were intimidated by this peculiar Englishman, or as if they'd been disconcerted by the author of *Miguel Street* and *A House for Mr. Biswas* when they met him in the flesh and had thought: Well, I didn't think it would be like this, or: This isn't the man I'd imagined, or: Nobody told me. So there he is, Naipaul, and it seems that all he can notice are outward movements, but in fact he's noticing inward movements too, although he interprets them in his own way, sometimes arbitrarily, and he's moving through

Buenos Aires in the year 1972 and writing as he moves or perhaps only wanting to write as his legs move through that strange city, and he's still young, forty years old, but he already has a considerable body of work behind him, a body of work that doesn't weigh him down or prevent him from moving briskly through Buenos Aires when he has an appointment to keep—the weight of the work, that's something to which we shall have to return, the weight and the pride that he takes in his work, the weight and the responsibility, which don't prevent his legs from moving nimbly or his hand from rising to hail a taxi, as he acts in character, like the man he is, a man who keeps his appointments punctually—but he *is* weighed down by the work when he goes strolling through Buenos Aires without appointments to exercise his British punctuality, without any pressing obligations, just walking along those strange avenues and streets, through that city in the southern hemisphere, so like the cities of the northern hemisphere, and yet nothing like them at all, a hole, a void that someone has suddenly inflated, a show that is strictly for local consumption; that's when he feels the weight of the work, and it's tiring to carry that weight as he walks, it exhausts him, it's irritating and shameful.

II.

Many years ago, before V. S. Naipaul—a writer whom I hold in high regard, by the way—won the Nobel Prize, I tried to write a story about him, with the title "Scholars of Sodom." The story began in Buenos Aires, where Naipaul had gone to write the long article on Eva Perón that was later included in a book published in Spain by Seix Barral in 1983. In the story, Naipaul arrived in Buenos Aires, I think it was his second visit to the city, and took a cab—and that's where I got stuck, which doesn't say much for my powers of imagination. I had some other scenes in mind that I didn't get around to writing. Mainly meetings and visits. Naipaul at newspaper offices. Naipaul at the home of a writer and political activist. Naipaul at the home of an upper-class literary lady. Naipaul making phone calls, returning to his hotel late at night, staying up and diligently making notes. Naipaul observing people. Sitting at a table in a famous café trying not to miss a single word. Naipaul visiting Borges. Naipaul returning to England and going through his notes. A brief but engaging account of the following series of events: the election of Perón's candidate, Perón's return, the election of Péron, the first symptoms of conflict within the Peronist camp, the right-wing armed groups, the Montoneros, the death of Perón, his widow's presidency, the indescribable López Rega, the army's position, violence flaring up again between right- and left-wing Peronists, the coup, the dirty war, the killings. But I might be getting all mixed up. Maybe Naipaul's article stopped before the coup; it probably came out before it was known how many had disappeared, before the scale of the atrocities was confirmed. In my story, Naipaul simply walked through the streets of Buenos Aires and somehow had a presentiment of the hell that would soon engulf the city. In that respect his article was prophetic, a modest, minor prophecy, nothing to match Sábato's *Abbadon the Exterminator*, but with a modicum of good will it could be seen as a member of the same family, a family of nihilist works paralyzed by horror. When I say "paralyzed," I mean it literally, not as a criticism. I'm thinking of the way some small boys freeze when suddenly confronted by an unforeseen horror, unable even to shut their eyes. I'm thinking of the way some girls have been known to die from a heart attack before the rapist has finished with them. Some literary artists are like those boys and girls. And that's how Naipaul was in my story, in spite of himself. He kept his eyes open and maintained his customary lucidity. He had what the Spanish call *bad milk*, a kind of spleen that immunized him against appeals to vulgar sentimentality. But in his nights of wandering around Buenos Aires, he, or his antennae, also picked up the static of hell. The problem was that he didn't know how to extract the messages from that noise, a predicament that certain writers, certain literary artists, find particularly unsettling. Naipaul's vision of Argentina could hardly have been less flattering. As the days went by, he came to find not only the city but the country as a whole insufferably aggravating. His uneasy feeling about the place seemed to be intensified by every visit, every new acquaintance he made. If I remember rightly, in my story Naipaul had arranged to meet Bioy Casares at a tennis club. Bioy didn't play any more, but he still went there to drink vermouth and chat with his friends and sit in the sun. The writer and his friends at the tennis club struck Naipaul as monuments to feeblemindedness, living illustrations of how a whole country could sink into imbecility. His meetings with journalists and politicians and union leaders left him with the same impression. After those exhausting days, Naipaul dreamed of Buenos Aires and the pampas, of Argentina as a whole, and his dreams invariably turned into nightmares. Argentineans are not especially popular in the rest of Latin America, but I can assure you that no Latin American has written a critique as devastating as Naipaul's. Not even a Chilean. Once, in a conversation with Rodrigo Fresán, I asked him what he thought of Naipaul's essay. Fresán, whose knowledge of literature in English is encyclopedic, barely remembered it, even though Naipaul is one of his favorite authors. But to get back to the story: Naipaul listens and notes down his impressions but mostly he walks around Buenos Aires. And suddenly, without giving the reader any sort of warning, he starts talking about sodomy. Sodomy as an Argentinean custom. Not just among homosexuals—in fact, now that I come think of it, I can't remember Naipaul mentioning homosexuality at all. He is talking about heterosexual relationships. You can imagine Naipaul, inconspicuously positioned in a bar (or a corner store—why not, since we're imagining), listening to the conversations of journalists, who start off by talking about politics, how the country has merrily set its course toward the abyss, and then, to cheer themselves up, they move on to amorous encounters, sexual conquests and lovers. All of their faceless lovers have at some point, Naipaul reminds himself, been sodomized. I took her up the ass, he writes. It's an act that in Europe, he reflects, would be regarded as shameful, or at least passed over in silence, but in the bars of Buenos Aires it's something to brag about, a sign of virility, of ultimate possession, since if you haven't fucked your lover or your girlfriend or your wife up the ass, you haven't really taken possession of her. And just as Naipaul is appalled by violence and thoughtlessness in politics, the sexual custom of "taking her up the ass," which he sees as a kind of violation, fills him ineluctably with disgust and contempt: a contempt of Argentineans that intensifies as the article proceeds. No one, it seems, is exempt from this pernicious custom. Well, no, there is one person quoted in the essay who rejects sodomy, though not with Naipaul's vehemence. The others, to a greater or lesser degree, accept and *practice* it, or have done so at some point, which leads Naipaul to conclude that Argentina is an unrepentantly macho country (whose machismo is thinly disguised by a dramaturgy of death and blood) and that in this hell of unfettered masculinity, Perón is the supermacho and Evita is the woman possessed, *totally* possessed. Any civilized society, thinks Naipaul, would condemn this sexual practice as aberrant and degrading, but not Argentina.

In the article or perhaps in my story, Naipaul is seized by an escalating vertigo. His strolls become the endless wanderings of a sleepwalker. He begins to feel queasy. It's as if, by their mere physical presence, the Argentineans he's visiting and talking to are causing a feeling of nausea that threatens to overwhelm him. He tries to find an explanation for their pernicious habit. And it's only logical, he thinks, to trace it back to the origins of the Argentinean people, descended from impoverished Spanish and Italian peasants. When those barbaric immigrants arrived on the pampas they brought their sexual practices along with their poverty. He seems to be satisfied with this explanation. In fact, it's so obvious that he accepts it as valid without further consideration. I remember that when I read the paragraph in which Naipaul explains what he takes to be the origin of the Argentinean habit of sodomy, I was somewhat taken aback. As well as being logically flawed, the explanation has no basis in historical or social facts. What did Naipaul know about the sexual customs of Spanish and Italian rural laborers from 1850 to 1925? Maybe, while touring the bars on Corrientes late one night, he heard a sportswriter recounting the sexual exploits of his grandfather or great-grandfather, who, when night fell over Sicily or Asturias, used to go fuck the sheep. Maybe. In my story, Naipaul closes his eyes and imagines a Mediterranean shepherd boy fucking a sheep or a goat. Then the shepherd boy caresses the goat and falls asleep. The shepherd boy dreams in the moonlight: he sees himself many years later, many pounds heavier, many inches taller, in possession of a large mustache, married, with numerous children, the boys working on the farm, tending the flock that has multiplied (or dwindled), the girls busy in the house or the garden, subjected to his molestations or to those of their brothers, and finally his wife, queen and slave, sodomized nightly, taken up the ass—a picturesque vignette that owes more to the erotico-bucolic desires of a nineteenth-century French pornographer than to harsh reality, which has the face of a castrated dog. I'm not saying that the good peasant couples of Sicily and Valencia *never* practiced sodomy, but surely not with the regularity of a custom destined to flourish beyond the seas. Now if Naipaul's immigrants had come from Greece, maybe the idea would merit consideration. Argentina might have been better off with a General Peronidis. Not much better off perhaps, but even so. Ah, if the Argentineans spoke Demotic. A Buenos Aires Demotic, combining the slangs of Piraeus and Salonica. With a gaucho Fierrescopulos, a faithful copy of Ulysses, and a Macedonio Hernandikis hammering the bed of Procrustes into shape. But, for better or for worse, Argentina is what it is and has the origins it has, which is to say, of this you may be sure, that it comes from everywhere but Paris.

THE ROOM NEXT DOOR

I was once, if I remember rightly, present at a gathering of madmen. Most of them were suffering from auditory hallucinations. A guy came up and asked if he could have a few words with me in private. We went to another room. The guy said that his medication was unhinging him. I'm getting more nervous every day, he said, And sometimes I have weird thoughts. That often happens, I told him. The guy said it was the first time it had happened to him. Then he rolled up the sleeves of his sweater and scratched his navel. He had a hand gun pushed into the top of his trousers. What's that? I asked him. It's my fucking belly button, said the guy: It itches and itches and what can I do? I'm scratching it all day long. Sure enough the skin around his navel was red and raw. I told him I didn't mean his navel, but what was below it. Is that a gun? I asked. Yes, it's a gun, said the guy, and he pulled it out and aimed it at the only window in the room. I considered asking if it was a fake, but I didn't. It looked real to me. I asked if I could have a look. Weapons aren't for loan, the guy said. It's like with cars and women. If you steal a car, you can lend it. Not something I'd recommend, but you can. The same if you're with a hooker. I wouldn't do it myself, I'd never lend any woman, but, you know, you could. When it comes to weapons, though, no way. And what if they're stolen or fakes? I asked him. Not even then. Once your fingerprints are on a weapon, you can't lend it. You understand? Sort of, I said. You have a commitment to the weapon, said the guy. In other words, you have to take care of it for the rest of your life, I said. Exactly, said the guy, you're married and that's all there is to it. You've got it pregnant with your fucking prints and that's all there is to it. Responsibility, said the guy. Then he raised his arm and aimed the gun straight at my head. I don't know if it was then or later that I thought of Moreau's *belle inertie*, or maybe I remembered having thought about it earlier, in a feverish and futile sort of way: beautiful inertia, the compositional procedure by which Moreau was able, in his canvases, to freeze, suspend and fix any scene, however hectic. I shut my eyes. I heard him asking me why I'd shut my eyes. Moreau's tranquility, some critics call it. Moreau's fear, say others who are less drawn to his work. Terror bedecked with jewels. I remembered his transparent pictures, his "unfinished" pictures, his gigantic, shadowy men, and his women, small in comparison to the masculine figures and inexpressibly beautiful. J. K. Huysmans wrote of his pictures: "An identical impression was created by these different scenes: that of a spiritual onanism, repeated in a chaste body." Spiritual onanism? Onanism period. All Moreau's giants and women, all the jewels, all the geometrical poise and splendor drop like paratroopers into the zone of chastity or responsibility. One night, when I was a sensitive young man of twenty, I overheard, in a boarding house in Guatemala, two men talking in the room next door. One of the voices was deep, the other was what you might call gravelly. At first, of course, I paid no attention to what they were saying. Both were Central Americans, though perhaps not from the same country, to judge from their intonation and turns of phrase. The guy with the gravelly voice started talking about a woman. He weighed up her beauty, the way she dressed and carried herself, her culinary skills. The guy with the deep voice agreed with everything he said. I imagined him lying on his bed, smoking, while the guy with the gravelly voice sat at the foot of the other bed, or maybe in the middle, with his shoes off, but still wearing his shirt and trousers. I didn't get the feeling they were friends; maybe they were sharing the room because they had no choice, or to save some money. They might have had dinner and some drinks together; that was probably as far as it went. But that was more than enough in Central America back then. I fell asleep several times while listening to them. Why didn't I sleep right through till the next morning? I don't know. Maybe I was too nervous. Maybe the voices from the other room got louder every now and then, and that was enough to wake me up. At one point the guy with the deep voice laughed. The guy with the gravelly voice said, or repeated, that he had killed his wife. I assumed that it was the woman he'd been praising before I fell asleep. I killed her, he said, and then he waited for the other guy to respond. It was a load off my mind. I did what was right. Nobody laughs at me. The guy with the deep voice shifted in his bed and said nothing. I imagined him with dark skin, with Indian and African blood, more African than Indian, a guy from Panama on his way home, maybe, or heading north to Mexico and the US border. After a long silence, during which all I could hear were strange noises, he asked the other guy if he was serious, if he'd really killed her. The guy with the gravelly voice said nothing; maybe he nodded. Then the black guy asked if he wanted a smoke. Why not, said the guy with gravelly voice, one more before we go to sleep. I didn't hear any more from them. The guy with the gravelly voice might have gotten up to switch off the light, while the black guy watched from his bed. I imagined a bedside table with an ashtray. A dark room, like mine, with a minuscule window that looked onto a dirt road. The guy with the gravelly voice was skinny and white, for sure. A nervous type. The other guy was black, big and solidly built, the sort of guy who doesn't often lose his cool. I stayed awake for a long time. When I reckoned they'd gone to sleep, I got up, trying not to make any noise, and switched on the light. I lit a cigarette and began to read. Dawn was infinitely distant. When I eventually started to feel sleepy again and switched off the light and stretched out on the bed, I heard something in the room next door. A woman's voice—it sounded like she had her lips to the wall—said Good night. Then I looked at my room, which, like the room next door, contained three beds, and I was afraid, and a scream rose in my throat, but I stifled it because I knew I had to.

LABYRINTH

They're seated. They're looking at the camera. They are, from left to right: J. Henric, J.-J. Goux, Ph. Sollers, J. Kristeva, M.-Th. Réveillé, P. Guyotat, C. Devade and M. Devade.

There's no photo credit.

They're sitting around a table. It's an ordinary table, made of wood, perhaps, or plastic, it could even be a marble table on metal legs, but nothing could be less germane to my purpose than to give an exhaustive description of it. The table is a table that is large enough to seat the above-mentioned individuals and it's in a café. Or appears to be. Let's suppose, for the moment, that it's in a café.

The eight people who appear in the photo, who are *posing* for the photo, are fanned out around one side of the table in a crescent or a kind of bent-open horseshoe, so that each of them can be seen clearly and completely. In other words, no one is facing away from the camera and no one is shown in profile. In front of them, or rather between them and the photographer (and this is slightly strange), there are three plants—a rhododendron, a ficus and an immortelle—rising from a planter, which may serve, but this is speculation, as a barrier between two quite distinct sections of the café.

The photo was probably taken in 1977 or thereabouts.

But let us return to the figures. On the left-hand side we have, as I said, J. Henric, that is, the writer Jacques Henric, born in 1938 and the author of *Archées*, *Artaud traversé par la Chine*, and *Chasses*. Henric is a solidly built man, broad-shouldered, muscular-looking, probably not very tall. He's wearing a checked shirt with the sleeves rolled halfway up his forearms. He's not what you would call a handsome man; he has the square face of a farmer or a construction worker, thick eyebrows and a dark chin, one of those chins that needs to be shaved twice a day (or so some people claim). His legs are crossed and his hands are clasped over his knee.

Next to him is J.-J. Goux. About J.-J. Goux I know nothing. He's probably called Jean-Jacques, but in this story, for the sake of convenience, I'll continue to use his initials. J.-J. Goux is young and blond. He's wearing glasses. There's nothing especially attractive about his features (although, compared to Henric, he looks not only more handsome but also more intelligent). The line of his jaw is symmetrical and his lips are full, the lower lip slightly thicker than the upper. He's wearing a turtleneck sweater and a dark leather jacket.

Beside J.-J. is Ph. Sollers, Philippe Sollers, born in 1936, the editor of *Tel Quel*, author of *Drame*, *Nombres*, and *Paradis*, a public figure familiar to everyone. Sollers has his arms crossed, the left arm resting on the surface of the table, the right arm resting on the left (and his right hand indolently cupping the elbow of his left arm). His face is round. It would be a gross exaggeration to say that it's the face of a fat man, but it probably will be in a few years' time: it's the face of a man who enjoys a good meal. An ironic, intelligent smile is hovering about his lips. His eyes, which are much livelier than those of Henric or J.-J., and smaller too, remain fixed on the camera, and the bags underneath them help to give his round face a look that is at once preoccupied, perky and playful. Like J.-J., he's wearing a turtleneck sweater, though the sweater that Sollers is wearing is white, dazzlingly white, while J.-J.'s is probably yellow or light green. Over the sweater Sollers is wearing a garment that appears at first glance to be a dark-colored leather jacket, though it could be made of a lighter material, possibly suede. He's the only one who's smoking.

Beside Sollers is J. Kristeva, Julia Kristeva, the Bulgarian semiologist, his wife. She is the author of *La traversée des signes*, *Pouvoirs de l'horreur*, and *Le langage, cet inconnu*. She's slim, with prominent cheekbones, black hair parted in the middle and gathered into a bun at the back. Her eyes are dark and lively, as lively as those of Sollers, although there are differences: as well as being larger, they transmit a certain hospitable warmth (that is, a certain serenity) which is absent from her husband's eyes. She's wearing just a turtleneck sweater, which is very close-fitting but the neck is loose, and a long V-shaped necklace that accentuates the form of her torso. At first glance she could almost be Vietnamese. Except that her breasts, it seems, are larger than those of the average Vietnamese woman. Hers is the only smile that allows us a glimpse of teeth.

Beside la Kristeva is M.-Th. Réveillé. About her too I know nothing. She's probably called Marie-Thérèse. Let's suppose that she is. Marie-Thérèse, then, is the first person so far not to be wearing a turtleneck sweater. Henric isn't either, actually, but his neck is short (he barely has a neck at all) while Marie-Thérèse Réveillé, by contrast, has a neck that is long and entirely revealed by the dark garment she is wearing. Her hair is straight and long, with a center part, light brown in color, or perhaps honey blonde. Thanks to the slight leftward turn of her face, a pearl can be seen suspended from her ear, like a stray satellite.

Next to Marie-Thérèse Réveillé is P. Guyotat, that is, Pierre Guyotat, born in 1940, the author of *Tombeau pour cinq cent mille soldats, Eden, Eden, Eden*, and *Prostitution*. Guyotat is bald. That's his most striking characteristic. He's also the most handsome man in the group. His bald head is radiant, his skull capacious and the black hair on his temples resembles nothing so much as the bay leaves that used to wreathe the heads of victorious Roman generals. Neither shrinking away nor striking a pose, he has the expression of a man who travels by night. He's wearing a leather jacket, a shirt and a T-shirt. The T-shirt (but here there must be some mistake) is white with black horizontal stripes and a thicker black stripe around the neck, like something a child might wear, or a Soviet parachutist. His eyebrows are narrow and definite. They mark the border between his immense forehead and a face that is wavering between concentration and indifference. The eyes are inquisitive, but perhaps they give a false impression. His lips are pressed together in a way that may not be deliberate.

Next to Guyotat is C. Devade. Caroline? Carole? Carla? Colette? Claudine? We'll never know. Let's say, for the sake of convenience, that she's called Carla Devade. She could well be the youngest member of the group. Her hair is short, without a fringe, and, although the photo is in black and white, it's reasonable to suppose that her skin has an olive tone, suggesting a Mediterranean background. Maybe Carla Devade is from the south of France, or Catalonia, or Italy. Only Julia Kristeva is as dark, but Kristeva's skin—although perhaps it's a trick of the light—has a metallic, bronze-like quality, while Carla Devade's is silky and yielding. She is wearing a dark sweater with a round neck, and a blouse. Her lips and her eyes betray more than a hint of a smile: a sign of recognition, perhaps.

Next to Carla Devade is M. Devade. This is presumably the writer Marc Devade, who was still a member of *Tel Quel*'s editorial committee in 1972. His relationship with Carla Devade is obvious: man and wife. Could they be brother and sister? Possibly, but the physical dissimilarities are numerous. Marc Devade (I find it hard to call him Marc, I would have preferred to translate that M into Marcel or Max) is blond, chubby-cheeked and has very light eyes. So it makes more sense to presume that they are man and wife. Just to be different, Devade is wearing a turtleneck sweater, like J.-J. Goux, Sollers and Kristeva, and a dark jacket. His eyes are large and beautiful, and his mouth is decisive. His hair, as I said, is blond; it's long (longer than that of the other men) and elegantly combed back. His forehead is broad and perhaps slightly bulging. And he has, although this may be an illusion produced by the graininess of the image, a dimple in his chin.

How many of them are looking directly at the photographer? Only half of the group: Henric, J.-J. Goux, Sollers and Marc Devade. Marie-Thérèse Réveillé and Carla Devade are looking away to the left, past Henric. Guyotat's gaze is angled slightly to the right, fixed on a point a yard or two from where the photographer is standing. And Kristeva, whose gaze is the strangest of all, appears to be looking straight at the camera, but in fact she's looking at the photographer's stomach, or to be more precise, into the empty space beside his hip.

The photo was taken in winter or autumn, or maybe at the beginning of spring, but certainly not in summer. Who are the most warmly dressed? J.-J. Goux, Sollers and Marc Devade, without question: they're wearing jackets over their turtleneck sweaters, and thick jackets too from the look of them, especially J.-J. and Devade's. Kristeva is a case apart: her turtleneck sweater is light, more elegant than practical, and she's not wearing anything over it. Then we have Guyotat. He might be as warmly dressed as the four I've already mentioned. He doesn't seem to be, but it's true that he's the only one wearing three layers: the black leather jacket, the shirt and the striped T-shirt. You could imagine him wearing those clothes even if the photo had been taken in summer. It's quite possible. All we can say for sure is that Guyotat is dressed as if he were on his way to somewhere else. As for Carla Devade, she's in between. Her blouse, whose collar is showing over the top of her sweater, looks soft and warm; the sweater itself is casual, but of good quality, neither very heavy nor very light. Finally we have Jacques Henric and Marie Thérèse Réveillé. Henric is clearly not a man who feels the cold, although his Canadian lumberjack's shirt looks warm enough. And the least warmly dressed of all is Marie-Thérèse Réveillé. Under her light, knitted, open-necked sweater there are only her breasts, cupped by a black or white bra.

All of them, more or less warmly dressed, captured by the camera at that moment in 1977 or thereabouts, are friends, and some of them are lovers too. For a start, Sollers and Kristeva, obviously, and the two Devades, Marc and Carla. Those, we might say, are the stable couples. And yet there are certain features of the photo (something about the arrangement of the objects, the petrified, musical rhododendron, two of its leaves invading the space of the ficus like clouds within a cloud, the grass growing in the planter, which looks more like fire than grass, the immortelle leaning whimsically to the left, the glasses in the center of the table, well away from the edges, except for Kristeva's, as if the other members of the group were worried they might fall) which suggest that there is a more complex and subtle web of relations among these men and women.

Let's imagine J.-J. Goux, for example, who is looking out at us through his thick submarine spectacles.

His space in the photo is momentarily vacant and we see him walking along Rue de l'École de Médecine, with books under his arm, of course, two books, till he comes out onto the Boulevard Saint-Germain. There he turns his steps toward the Mabillon metro station, but first he stops in front of a bar, checks the time, goes in and orders a cognac. After a while J.-J. moves away from the bar and sits down at a table near the window. What does he do? He opens a book. We can't tell what book it is, but we do know that he's finding it difficult to concentrate. Every twenty seconds or so he lifts his head and looks out onto the Boulevard Saint-Germain, his gaze a little more gloomy each time. It's raining and people are walking hurriedly under their open umbrellas. J.-J.'s blond hair isn't wet, from which we can deduce that it began to rain after he entered the bar. It's getting dark. J.-J. remains seated in the same place, and now there are two cognacs and two coffees on his tab. Coming closer we can see that the dark rings under his eyes have the look of a war zone. At no point has he taken off his glasses. He's a pitiful sight. After a very long wait, he goes back out onto the street where he is gripped by a shiver, perhaps because of the cold. For a moment he stands still on the sidewalk and looks both ways, then he starts walking in the direction of the Mabillon metro station. When he reaches the entrance, he runs his hand through his hair several times, as if he'd suddenly realized that his hair was a mess, although it's not. Then he goes down the steps and the story ends or freezes in an empty space where appearances gradually fade away. Who was J.-J. Goux waiting for? Someone he's in love with? Someone he was hoping to sleep with that night? And how was his delicate sensibility affected by that person's failure to show up?

Let's suppose that the person who didn't come was Jacques Henric. While J.-J. was waiting for him, Henric was riding a 250-cc Honda motorbike to the entrance of the apartment building where the Devades live. But no. That's impossible. Let's imagine that Henric simply climbed onto his Honda and rode away into a vaguely literary, vaguely unstable Paris, and that his absence on this occasion is strategic, as amorous absences nearly always are.

So let's set up the couples again. Carla Devade and Marc Devade. Sollers and Kristeva. J.-J. Goux and Jacques Henric. Marie-Thérèse Réveillé and Pierre Guyotat. And let's set up the night. J.-J. Goux is sitting and reading a book whose title is immaterial, in a bar on the Boulevard Saint-Germain; his turtleneck sweater won't let his skin breathe, but he doesn't yet feel entirely ill at ease. Henric is stretched out on his bed, half undressed, smoking and looking at the ceiling. Sollers is shut up in his study, writing (pinkly snug and warm inside his turtleneck sweater). Julia Kristeva is at the university. Marie-Thérèse Réveillé is walking along Avenue de Friedland near the intersection with Rue Balzac, and the headlights of cars are shining in her face. Guyotat is in a bar on Rue Lacépède, near the Jardin des Plantes, drinking with some friends. Carla Devade is in her apartment, sitting on a chair in the kitchen, doing nothing. Marc Devade is at the *Tel Quel* office, speaking politely on the phone to one of the poets he most admires and hates. Soon Sollers and Kristeva will be together, reading after dinner. They will not make love tonight. Soon Marie-Thérèse Réveillé and Guyotat will be together in bed, and he will sodomize her. They will fall asleep at five in the morning, after exchanging a few words in the bathroom. Soon Carla Devade and Marc Devade will be together, and she will shout, and he will shout, and she will go to the bedroom and pick up a novel, any one of the many that are lying on her bedside table, and he will sit at his desk and try to write but he won't be able to. Carla will fall asleep at one in the morning, Marc at half-past two, and they will try not to touch each other. Soon Jacques Henric will go down to the underground parking lot and climb onto his Honda and venture out into the cold streets of Paris, becoming cold himself, a man who shapes his own destiny, and knows, or at least believes, that he is lucky. He will be the only member of the group to see the day dawning, with the disastrous retreat of the last night wanderers, each an enigmatic letter in an imaginary alphabet. Soon J.-J. Goux, who was the first to fall asleep, will have a dream in which a photo will appear, and he'll hear a voice warning him of the devil's presence and of hapless death. He'll wake with a start from this dream or auditory nightmare and won't be able to get back to sleep for the rest of the night.

Day breaks and the photo is illuminated once again. Marie-Thérèse Réveillé and Carla Devade look off to the left, at an object beyond Henric's muscular shoulders. There is recognition or acceptance in Carla's gaze: that much is clear from her half-smile and gentle eyes. Marie-Thérèse, however, has a penetrating gaze: her lips are slightly open, as if she were having difficulty breathing, and her eyes are trying to fix on (trying, unsuccessfully, to *nail*) the object of her attention, which is presumably moving. Both women are looking in the same direction, but it's clear that they have quite different emotional reactions to whatever it is they are seeing. Carla's gentleness may be conditioned by ignorance. Marie-Thérèse's insecurity, her defensive yet inquisitorial glare, may result from the sudden stripping away of various layers of experience.

Any moment now, J.-J. Goux might start to cry. The voice that warned him of the devil's presence is still ringing, though faintly, in his ears. He is not, however, looking to the left, at the object that has attracted the women's attention, but directly at the camera, and an infinitesimal smile is creeping over his lips, a would-be ironic smile confined, for the moment, to the safer domain of placidity.

When night falls over the photograph again, J.-J. Goux will

head straight for his apartment, make himself a sandwich, watch television for exactly fifteen minutes, not one more, then sit in an armchair in the living room and call Philippe Sollers. The phone will ring five times and J.-J. will hang up slowly, holding the receiver in his right hand, raising his left hand to his lips, and touching them with two fingers, as if to check that he's still there, that the person there is *him*, in a living room that's not too big, not too small, crowded with books, and dark.

As for Carla Devade, having lost her acquiescent smile, she'll call Marie-Thérèse Réveillé, who will pick up the phone after three rings. In a roundabout way, they'll talk about things they don't really want to talk about at all, and arrange to meet in three days' time at a café on Rue Galande. Tonight Marie-Thérèse will go out on her own, with nowhere in particular to go, and Carla will shut herself in her room as soon as she hears the sound of Marc Devade's key sliding into the lock. But for now nothing tragic will happen. Marc Devade will read an essay by a Bulgarian linguist; Guyotat will go to see a film by Jacques Rivette; Julia Kristeva will stay up late reading; Philippe Sollers will stay up late writing, and he and his wife will barely exchange a few words, shut away in their respective studies; Jacques Henric will sit down at his typewriter but nothing will occur to him, so after twenty minutes he'll put on his leather jacket and his boots and go down to the underground parking garage and look for his Honda in the dark; for some reason the lights in the parking lot don't seem to be working, but Henric can remember where he left his bike, so he walks in the dark, in the belly of that whale-like parking lot, without fear or apprehension of any kind, until about halfway there he hears an unusual noise (not a knocking in the pipes or the noise of a car door opening or closing) and he stops, without really understanding why, and listens, but the noise is not repeated, and now the silence is absolute.

And then the night ends (or a small part of the night, at least, a manageable part) and light wraps the photo like a bandage on fire, and there he is again, Pierre Guyotat, almost a familiar presence now, with his powerful, shiny bald head and his leather jacket, the jacket of an anarchist or a commissar from the Spanish Civil War, and his sidelong gaze, veering off to the right, as if into the space behind the photographer, as if directed at someone near or at the bar, perhaps, standing or sitting on a stool, someone whose back is turned to Guyotat and whose face would be invisible to him unless, and this is not unlikely, there is a mirror behind the bar. It may be a woman. A young woman, maybe. Guyotat looks at her reflection in the mirror and looks at the back of her neck. Guyotat's gaze, however, is far less intense than the gaze of this woman, which is plumbing an abyss. Here we can reasonably conclude that, while Guyotat is looking at a stranger, Marie-Thérèse and Carla are looking at a man they know, although, as is usually (or, in fact, inevitably) the case, their perceptions of him are entirely different.

Let's call these two beyond the frame X and Z. X is the woman at the bar. Z is the man who is known to Marie-Thérèse and Carla. They don't know him very well, of course. From Carla's gaze (which is not only gentle but protective) it could be inferred that he is young, although from Marie-Thérèse's gaze it could also be inferred that he is a potentially dangerous individual. Who else knows Z? No one, or at least there is nothing to suggest that his presence is of any concern to the others. Maybe he's a young writer who at some stage has tried to get his work published in *Tel Quel*; maybe he's a young journalist from South America—no, from Central America—who at some point tried to write an article about the group. He may well be an ambitious young man. If he's a Central American in Paris, as well as ambitious, he may well be bitter. Of the people sitting around the table, he knows only Marie-Thérèse, Carla, Sollers and Marc Devade. Let's say he once visited the *Tel Quel* office and was introduced to those four (he also once shook hands with Marcelin Pleynet, but Pleynet's not in the photo). He has never seen the others in his life, or only (in the cases of Guyotat and Jacques Henric) in author photos. So we can imagine the young Central American, hungry and bitter, in the *Tel Quel* office, and we can imagine Philippe Sollers and Marc Devade, wavering between puzzlement and indifference as they listen to him, and we can even imagine that Carla Devade is there by pure chance; she has come to meet her husband, she has brought some papers that Marc left behind on his desk, she's there because she couldn't stand being alone in the apartment a minute longer, etc. What we can't imagine (or justify) in any way at all is Marie-Thérèse's presence in the office. She is Guyotat's partner, she doesn't work for *Tel Quel* and she has no reason to be there. And yet there she is and that is where she meets the young Central American. Is she there on that day because of Carla Devade? Has Carla arranged to meet Marie-Thérèse at the office because she knows that Marc will not be coming home with her? Or has Marie-Thérèse come to meet someone else? Let's return, discreetly, to the afternoon when the Central American came to the office on Rue Jacob to pay his respects.

It's the end of the working day. The secretary has already gone home, and when the bell rings it's Marc Devade who opens the door and lets the visitor in without meeting his eye. The Central American crosses the threshold and follows Marc Devade to an office at the end of the corridor. He leaves a trail of drops on the wooden floor behind him, although it stopped raining quite some time ago. Devade is, of course, oblivious to this detail; he walks ahead talking about something or other—the weather, money, chores—with that elegance that only certain Frenchmen seem to possess. In the office, which is spacious, and contains a desk, several chairs, two armchairs, and shelves full of books and magazines, Sollers is waiting, and as soon as the introductions are over the Central American hails him as a genius, one of the century's most brilliant minds, a compliment that would be par for the course in certain tropical nations on the far side of the Atlantic but which, in the *Tel Quel* office and the ears of Philippe Sollers, verges on the preposterous. In fact, as soon as the Central American makes his declaration, Sollers catches Devade's eye and both of them are wondering whether they've let a madman in. Deep down, however, Sollers is eighty per cent in agreement with the Central American's appraisal, so once he has set aside the idea that the visitor might be mocking him, the conversation proceeds in an amicable fashion, at least for a start. The Central American speaks of Julia Kristeva (and winks at Sollers as he mentions that eminent Bulgarian), he speaks of Marcelin Pleynet (whom he has already met), and of Denis Roche (whose work he claims to be translating). Devade listens to him with a slightly wry smile. Sollers listens, nodding from time to time, his boredom increasing with every passing second. Suddenly, a sound of steps in the corridor. The door opens. Carla Devade appears, wearing tight corduroy trousers, flat shoes and a disconsolate smile on her pretty Mediterranean face. Marc Devade gets up from his chair; for a moment the couple whisper questions and answers. The Central American has fallen silent; Sollers is mechanically flipping through an English magazine. Then Carla and Marc walk across the room (Carla taking tentative little steps, holding her husband's arm), the Central American stands up, is introduced, and obsequiously greets the newcomer. The conversation is immediately resumed, but the Central American's chatter veers off in a new direction, unfortunately for him (he changes the subject from literature to the matchless beauty and grace of French women), at which point Sollers completely loses interest. Shortly afterward, the visit is brought to a close: Sollers looks at his watch, says it's late; Devade shows the Central American to the door, shakes his hand, and the visitor, instead of waiting for the elevator, rushes down the stairs. On the second-floor landing he runs into Marie-Thérèse Réveillé. The Central American is talking to himself in Spanish, not under his breath but out loud. As their paths cross, Marie-Thérèse notices a fierce look in his eyes. They bump into each other. Both apologize. They look at each other again (and this is surprising, the way their eyes meet again *after* the apology), and what she sees, beneath the expedient mask of bitterness, is a well of unbearable horror and fear.

So the Central American, Z, is there in the café when the photo is taken, and Carla and Marie-Thérèse have recognized him, they've remembered him; perhaps he has just arrived, perhaps he walked past the table at which the group is sitting and greeted them, but except for the two women, they had no idea who he was; this happens quite often, of course, but it's something that the Central American still can't accept with equanimity. There he is, to the left of the group, with some Central American friends, or waiting for them, maybe, and deep within him—nourished by affronts and grudges, fuelled by bitterness and the chill of the City of Light—there's a seething. His appearance, however, is equivocal: it makes Carla Devade feel like a protective older sister or a missionary nun in Africa, but it catches at Marie-Thérèse Réveillé like barbed wire and triggers a vague erotic longing.

And then night falls again and the photo empties out or disappears under a scribble of lines entirely traced by the night's mechanism, and Sollers is writing in his study, and Kristeva is writing in the study next door, soundproofed studies so they can't hear each other typing, for example, or getting up to consult a book, or coughing or talking to themselves, and Carla and Marc Devade are leaving a cinema (they've been to a film by Rivette), not talking to each other, although, a couple of times, Marc and then Carla, who's more distracted, greet people they know, and J.-J. Goux is preparing his dinner, a frugal dinner consisting of bread, pâté, cheese and a glass of wine, and Guyotat is undressing Marie-Thérèse Réveillé and throwing her onto the sofa with a violent thrust that Marie-Thérèse intercepts in midair as if she were catching a butterfly of lucidity in a net of lucidity, and Henric is leaving his apartment, going down to the parking lot and he stops again as the lights go out, first the ones near the metal roller gate that opens onto the street, and then the others, till there is only the light down at the back, flickering helplessly, illuminating his multicolored Honda, and then it fails as well. And it occurs to Henric that his motorbike is like an Assyrian god, but for the moment his legs refuse to walk on into the darkness, and Marie-Thérèse shuts her eyes and opens her legs, one foot on the sofa, the other on the carpet, while Guyotat pushes into her, the panties still around her thighs, and calls her his little whore, his little bitch, and asks her what she did all day, what happened to her, what streets she wandered down, and J.-J. Goux is sitting at the table and spreading pâté on a piece of bread and lifting it to his mouth and chewing, first on the right side, then on the left, unhurriedly, with a book by Robert Pinget open beside him at page two and the television switched off but the screen reflecting his image, a man on his own with his mouth closed and his cheeks full, looking thoughtful and absent, and Carla Devade and Marc Devade are making love, Carla on top, illuminated only by the light in the corridor, a light they usually leave on, and Carla is groaning and trying not to look at her husband's face, his blond hair in a mess now, his light eyes, his broad and placid face, his delicate, elegant

hands, devoid of the fire she's longing for, ineffectually holding her hips, as if he were trying to keep her there with him,
but he has no real sense of what she might be fleeing from or
what her flight might mean, a flight that goes on and on like
torture, and Kristeva and Sollers are going to bed, first her, she
has to lecture early the next day, then him, and both of them
take books that they will leave on their bedside tables when
sleep comes to close their eyes, and Philippe Sollers will dream
that he is walking along a beach in Brittany with a scientist
who has discovered a way to destroy the world; they will be
walking westward along this long, deserted beach, bounded by
rocks and black cliffs, and suddenly Sollers will realize that the
scientist (who is talking and explaining) is himself and that the
man walking beside him is a murderer; this will dawn on him
when he looks down at the wet sand (with its soup-like consis-
tency) and the crabs skittering away to hide and the prints the
two of them are leaving on the beach (there is a certain logic
to this: identifying the murderer by his footprints), and Julia
Kristeva will dream of a little village in Germany where years
ago she participated in a seminar, and she'll see the streets of
the village, clean and empty, and sit down in a square that's
tiny but full of plants and trees, and close her eyes and listen
to the distant cheeping of a single bird and wonder if the bird
is in a cage or free, and she'll feel a breeze on her neck and her
face, neither cold nor warm, a perfect breeze, perfumed with
lavender and orange blossom, and then she'll remember her
seminar and look at her watch, but it will have stopped.

So the Central American is outside the frame of the photograph, sharing that pristine and deceptive territory with the
object of Guyotat's gaze: an unknown woman armed only, for
the moment, with her beauty. Their eyes will not meet. They
will pass each other by like shadows, briefly sharing the same
hazardous ambit: the itinerant theater of Paris. The Central

American could quite easily become a murderer. Perhaps, back in his country, he will, but not here, where the only blood he could possibly shed is his own. This Pol Pot won't kill anyone in Paris. And actually, back in Tegucigalpa or San Salvador, he'll probably end up teaching in a university. As for the unknown woman, she will not be captured by Guyotat's asbestos nets. She's at the bar, waiting for the boyfriend she'll marry before long (him or the next one), and their marriage will be disastrous, though not without its moments of comfort. Literature brushes past these literary creatures and kisses them on the lips, but they don't even notice.

The section of restaurant or café that contains the photo's nest of smoke continues imperturbably on its voyage through nothingness. Behind Sollers, for instance, we can make out the fragmentary figures of three men. None of the faces can be seen in its entirety. The man on the left, in profile: a forehead, one eyebrow, the back part of his ear, the top of his head. The man on the right: a little piece of his forehead, his cheekbone, strands of dark hair. The man in the middle, who seems to be calling the tune: most of his forehead, traversed by two clearly visible wrinkles, his eyebrows, the bridge of his nose, and a discreet quiff. Behind them, there is a pane of glass and behind the glass many people walking about curiously among stalls or exhibition stands, bookstands perhaps, mostly facing away from our characters (who have their backs to them in turn), except for a child with a round face and straight bangs, wearing a jacket that may be too small for him, looking sideways toward the café, as if from that distance he could observe everything going on inside, which, on the face of it, seems rather unlikely.

And in a corner, to the right: the waiting man, the listening man. His face appears just above Marc Devade's blond hair. His hair is dark and abundant, his eyebrows are thick, he is thin. In one hand (a hand resting listlessly against his right temple), he is holding a cigarette. A spiral of smoke is rising from the cigarette toward the ceiling, and the camera has captured it almost as if it were the image of a ghost. Telekinesis. An expert could identify the brand of cigarette that he's smoking in half a second just by the solid look of that smoke. Gauloises, no doubt. He's gazing off toward the photo's right-hand side—that is, he's pretending not to know that the photo is being taken, but in a way he too is posing.

And there is yet another person: careful examination reveals something protruding from Guyotat's neck like a cancerous growth, which turns out to be made up of a nose, a withered forehead, the outline of an upper lip, the profile of a man who is looking, with a certain gravity, in the same direction as the smoking man, although their gazes could not be more different.

And then the photo is occluded and all that is left is the smoke of a Gauloise floating in the air, as if the viewfinder had suddenly swung to the right, toward the black hole of chance, and Sollers comes to a sudden halt in the street, a street near the Place Wagram, and feels in his pockets as if he had left his address book behind or lost it, and Marie-Thérèse Réveillé is driving on the Boulevard Malesherbes, near the Place Wagram, and J.-J. Goux is talking on the phone with Marc Devade (J.-J.'s voice is unsteady, Devade isn't saying a word), and Guyotat and Henric are walking on Rue Saint-André des Arts, heading for Rue Dauphine, and by chance they run into Carla Devade who says hello and joins them, and Julia Kristeva is coming out of class surrounded by a retinue of students, quite a few of whom are foreign (two Spaniards, a Mexican, an Italian, two Germans), and once more the photo dissolves into nothingness.

Aurora borealis. Terrible dawn. As they open their eyes, they are almost transparent. Marc Devade, alone in bed, snug in gray pajamas, dreaming of the Académie Goncourt. J.-J. Goux at his window, watching clouds float through the sky over Paris and comparing them unfavorably to certain clouds in paintings by Pisarro or the clouds in his nightmare. Julia Kristeva is sleeping and her calm face seems an Assyrian mask until, with a very slight wince of discomfort, she wakes. Philippe Sollers is in the kitchen, leaning on the edge of the sink, and blood is dripping from his right index finger. Carla Devade is climbing the stairs to her apartment after having spent the night with Guyotat. Marie-Thérèse Réveillé is making coffee and reading a book.

Jacques Henric is walking through a dark parking garage, which echoes to the sound of his boots on the cement.

A world of forms is unfolding before his eyes, a world of distant noises. The possibility of fear is approaching the way wind approaches a provincial capital. Henric stops, his heart speeds up, he tries to orient himself. Before, he could at least glimpse shadows and silhouettes at the far end of the parking lot; now it seems hermetically black, like the darkness in an empty coffin at the bottom of a crypt. So he decides to keep still. In that stillness, his heartbeat gradually slows and memory brings back images of the day. He remembers Guyotat, whom he secretly admires, openly pursuing little Carla. Once again, he sees them smiling and then he sees them walking away down a street where yellow lights scatter and regroup sporadically, without any obvious pattern, although Henric knows deep down that everything is determined in some way, everything is causally linked to something else, and human nature leaves very little room for the truly gratuitous. He touches his crotch. He is startled by this movement, the first he has made for some time. He has an erection and yet he doesn't feel sexually aroused in any way.

THE VAGARIES OF THE LITERATURE
OF DOOM

It's odd that it was bourgeois writers who transported José Hernández's *Martín Fierro* to the center of the Argentine canon. The point is debatable, of course, but the truth is that Fierro, the gaucho, paradigm of the dispossessed, of the brave man (but also of the thug), presides over a canon, the Argentine canon, that only keeps getting stranger. As a poem, *Martín Fierro* is nothing out of this world. As a novel, however, it's alive, full of meanings to explore, which means that the wind still gusts (or blasts) through it, it still smells of the out-of-doors, it still cheerfully accepts the blows of fate. Nevertheless, it's a novel of freedom and squalor, not of good breeding and manners. It's a novel about bravery rather than intelligence, let alone morality.

If *Martín Fierro* dominates Argentine literature and its place is in the center of the canon, the work of Borges, probably the greatest writer born in Latin America, is only a footnote.

It's odd that Borges wrote so much and so well about *Martín Fierro*. Not just the young Borges, who can be nationalistic at times, if only on the page, but also the adult Borges, who is occasionally thrown into ecstasies (strange ecstasies, as if he were contemplating the gestures of the Sphinx) by the four most memorable scenes in Hernández's work, and who sometimes even writes perfect, listless stories with plots imitative of Hernández's. When Borges recalls Hernández, it's not with the affection and admiration with which he refers to Güiraldes, or with the surprise and resignation evoked by Evaristo Carriego, that familiar bogeyman. With Hernández, or with *Martín Fierro*, Borges seems to be acting, acting to perfection, in fact, but in a play that strikes him from the beginning as not so much odious as wrongheaded. And yet, odious or wrongheaded, it also seems to him inevitable. In this sense, his silent death in Geneva is highly eloquent. More than eloquent. In fact, his death in Geneva talks a blue streak.

With Borges alive, Argentine literature becomes what most readers think of as Argentine literature. That is: there's Macedonio Fernández, who at times resembles the Valéry of Buenos Aires; there's Güiraldes, who's rich and ailing; there's Ezequiel Martínez Estrada; there's Marechal, who later turns Peronist; there's Mujica Láinez; there's Bioy Casares, who writes Latin America's first and best fantastic novel, though all the writers of Latin America rush to deny it; there's Bianco; there's Mallea, the pedant; there's Silvina Ocampo; there's Sábato; there's Cortázar, best of them all; there's Roberto Arlt, most hard done by. When Borges dies, everything suddenly comes to an end. It's as if Merlin had died, though Buenos Aires' literary circles aren't exactly Camelot. Gone, most of all, is the reign of balance. Apollonian intelligence gives way to Dionysian desperation. Sleep, an often hypocritical, false, accommodating, cowardly sleep, becomes nightmare, a nightmare that's often honest, loyal, brave, a nightmare that operates without a safety net, but a nightmare in the end, and, what's worse, a literary nightmare, literary suicide, a literary dead end.

And yet with the passage of the years it's fair to ask whether the nightmare, or the skin of the nightmare, is really as radical as its exponents proclaimed. Many of them live much better than I do. In this sense, I can say that I'm an Apollonian rat and they're starting to look more and more like angora or Siamese cats neatly deflead by a collar labeled Acme or Dionysius, which at this point in history amounts to the same thing.

Regrettably, Argentine literature today has three reference points. Two are public. The third is secret. All three are in some sense reactions against Borges. All three ultimately represent a step backward and are conservative, not revolutionary, although all three, or at least two of them, have set themselves up as leftist alternatives.

The first is the fiefdom of Osvaldo Soriano, who was a good minor novelist. When it comes to Soriano, you have to have a brain full of fecal matter to see him as someone around whom a literary movement can be built. I don't mean he's bad. As I've said: he's good, he's fun, he's essentially an author of crime novels or something vaguely like crime novels, whose main virtue—praised at length by the always perceptive Spanish critical establishment—is his sparing use of adjectives, a restraint lost, in any case, after his fourth or fifth book. Hardly the basis for a school. Apart from Soriano's kindness and generosity, which are said to be great, I suspect that his sway is due to sales, to his accessibility, his mass readership, although to speak of a mass readership when we're really talking about twenty thousand people is clearly an exaggeration. What Argentine writers have learned from Soriano is that they, too, can make money. No need to write original books, like Cortázar or Bioy, or total novels, like Cortázar or Marechal, or perfect stories, like Cortázar or Bioy, and no need, especially, to squander your time and health in a lousy library when you're never going to win a Nobel Prize anyway. All you have to do is write like Soriano. A little bit of humor, lots of Buenos Aires solidarity and camaraderie, a dash of tango, a worn-out boxer or two, an old but solid Marlowe. But, sobbing, I ask myself on my knees, solid where? Solid in heaven, solid in the toilet of your literary agent? What kind of nobody are you, anyway? You have an agent? And an Argentine agent, no less?

If the Argentine writer answers this last question in the affirmative, we can be sure that he won't write like Soriano but like Thomas Mann, like the Thomas Mann of *Faust*. Or, dizzied by the vastness of the pampa, like Goethe himself.

The second line of descent is more complex. It begins with Roberto Arlt, though it's likely that Arlt is totally innocent of this mess. Let's say, to put it modestly, that Arlt is Jesus Christ. Argentina is Israel, of course, and Buenos Aires is Jerusalem. Arlt is born and lives a rather short life, dying at forty-two, if I'm not mistaken. He's a contemporary of Borges. Borges is born in 1899 and Arlt in 1900. But unlike Borges, Arlt grows up poor, and as an adolescent he goes to work instead of to Geneva. Arlt's most frequently held job was as a reporter, and it's in the light of the newspaper trade that one views many of his virtues, as well as his defects. Arlt is quick, bold, malleable, a born survivor, but he's also an autodidact, though not an autodidact in the sense that Borges was: Arlt's apprenticeship proceeds in disorder and chaos, through the reading of terrible translations, in the gutter rather than the library. Arlt is a Russian, a character out of Dostoyevsky, whereas Borges is an Englishman, a character out of Chesterton or Shaw or Stevenson. Sometimes, despite himself, Borges even seems like a character out of Kipling. In the war between the literary factions of Boedo and Florida, Arlt is with Boedo, although my impression is that his thirst for battle was never excessive. His oeuvre consists of two story collections and three novels, though in fact he wrote four novels, and his uncollected stories, stories that appeared in newspapers and magazines and that Arlt could write while he talked about women with his fellow reporters, would fill at least two more books. He's also the author of a volume of newspaper columns called *Aguafuertes porteños* [Etchings from Buenos Aires], in the best French impressionist tradition, and *Aguafuertes españoles* [Etchings from Spain], sketches of daily life in Spain in the 1930s, which are full of gypsies, the poor, and the benevolent. He tried to get rich through deals that had nothing to do with the Argentine literature of the day, though they did have something to do with science fiction, and they were always categorical failures. Then he died and, as he would have said, that was the end of everything.

But it wasn't the end of everything, because like Jesus Christ, Arlt had his St. Paul. Arlt's St. Paul, the founder of his church, is Ricardo Piglia. I often ask myself: What would have happened if Piglia, instead of falling in love with Arlt, had fallen in love with Gombrowicz? Why didn't Piglia devote himself to spreading the Gombrowiczian good news, or specialize in Juan Emar, the Chilean writer who bears a marked resemblance to the monument to the unknown soldier? A mystery. In any case, it's Piglia who raises up Arlt in his own coffin soaring over Buenos Aires, in a very Piglian or Arltian scene, though one that takes place only in Piglia's imagination, not in reality. It wasn't a crane that lowered Arlt's coffin. The stairs were wide enough for the job. The body in the box wasn't a heavyweight champion's.

By this I don't mean to say that Arlt is a bad writer, because in fact he's an excellent writer, nor do I mean to say that Piglia is a bad writer, because I think Piglia is one of the best Latin American novelists writing today. The problem is, I find it hard to stand the nonsense—thuggish nonsense, doomy nonsense—that Piglia knits around Arlt, who's probably the only innocent person in this whole business. I can in no way condone bad translators of Russian, as Nabokov said to Edmund Wilson while mixing his third martini, and I can't accept plagiarism as one of the arts. Seen as a closet or a basement, Arlt's work is fine. Seen as the main room of the house, it's a macabre joke. Seen as the kitchen, it promises food poisoning. Seen as the bathroom, it'll end up giving us scabies. Seen as the library, it's a guarantee of the destruction of literature.

Or in other words: the literature of doom has to exist, but if nothing else exists, it's the end of literature.

Like solipsistic literature—so in vogue in Europe now that the young Henry James is again roaming about at will—a literature of the I, of extreme subjectivity, of course must and should exist. But if all writers were solipsists, literature would turn into the obligatory military service of the mini-me or into a river of autobiographies, memoirs, journals that would soon become a cesspit, and then, again, literature would cease to exist. Because who really cares about the sentimental meanderings of a professor? Who can say, without lying through his teeth, that the daily routine of a dreary professor in Madrid, no matter how distinguished, is more interesting than the nightmares and dreams and ambitions of the celebrated and ridiculous Carlos Argentino Daneri? No one with half a brain. Listen: I don't have anything against autobiographies, so long as the writer has a penis that's twelve inches long when erect. So long as the writer is a woman who was once a whore and is moderately wealthy in her old age. So long as the author of the tome in question has lived a remarkable life. It goes without saying that if I had to choose between the solipsists and the bad boys of the literature of doom I'd take the latter. But only as a lesser evil.

The third lineage in play in contemporary or post-Borgesian Argentine literature is the one that begins with Osvaldo Lamborghini. This is the secret current. It's as secret as the life of Lamborghini, who died in Barcelona in 1985, if I'm not mistaken, and who left as literary executor his most beloved disciple, César Aira, which is like a rat naming a hungry cat as executor.

If Arlt, who as a writer is the best of the three, is the basement of the house that is Argentine literature, and Soriano is a vase in the guest room, Lamborghini is a little box on a shelf in the basement. A little cardboard box, covered in dust. And if you open the box, what you find inside is hell. Forgive me for being so melodramatic. I always have the same problem with Lamborghini. There's no way to describe his work without falling into hyperbole. The word *cruelty* fits it like a glove. *Harshness* does too, but especially *cruelty.* The unsuspecting reader may glimpse the sort of sadomasochistic game of writing workshops that charitable souls with pedagogical inclinations organize in insane asylums. Perhaps, but that doesn't go far enough. Lamborghini is always two steps ahead of (or behind) his pursuers.

It's strange to think about Lamborghini now. He died at forty-five, which means that I'm four years older than he was then. Sometimes I pick up one of his two books, edited by Aira—which is only a figure of speech, since they might just as well have been edited by the linotypist or by the doorman at his publishing house in Barcelona, Serbal—and I can hardly read it, not because I think it's bad but because it scares me, especially all of *Tadeys*, an excruciating novel, which I read (two or three pages at a time, not a page more) only when I feel especially brave. Few books can be said to smell of blood, spilled guts, bodily fluids, unpardonable acts.

Today, when it's so fashionable to talk about nihilists (although what's usually meant by this is Islamic terrorists, who aren't nihilists at all), it isn't a bad idea to take a look at the work of a real nihilist. The problem with Lamborghini is that he ended up in the wrong profession. He should have gone to work as a hit man, or a prostitute, or a gravedigger, which are less complicated jobs than trying to destroy literature. Literature is an armor-plated machine. It doesn't care about writers. Sometimes it doesn't even notice they exist. Literature's enemy is something else, something much bigger and more powerful, that in the end will conquer it. But that's another story.

Lamborghini's friends are fated to plagiarize him ad nauseam, something that might—if he could see them vomit—make Lamborghini himself happy. They're also fated to write badly, horribly, except for Aira, who maintains a gray, uniform prose that, sometimes, when he's faithful to Lamborghini, crystallizes into memorable works, like the story "Cecil Taylor" or the novella *How I Became a Nun*, but that in its neo-avant-garde and Rousselian (and utterly acritical) drift, is mostly just boring. Prose that devours itself without finding a way to move forward. A criticism that translates into the acceptance—qualified, of course—of that tropical figure, the professional Latin American writer, who always has a word of praise for anyone who asks for it.

Of these three lineages—the three strongest in Argentine literature, the three departure points of the literature of doom—I'm afraid that the one which will triumph is the one that most faithfully represents the sentimental rabble, in the words of Borges. The sentimental rabble is no longer the Right (largely because the Right busies itself with publicity and the joys of cocaine and the plotting of currency devaluations and starvation, and in literary matters is functionally illiterate or settles for reciting lines from *Martín Fierro*) but the Left, and what the Left demands of its intellectuals is soma, which is exactly what it receives from its masters. Soma, soma, soma Soriano, forgive me, yours is the kingdom.

Arlt and Piglia are another story. Let's call theirs a love affair and leave them in peace. Both of them—Arlt without a doubt—are an important part of Argentine and Latin American literature, and their fate is to ride alone across the ghost-ridden pampa. But that's no basis for a school.

Corollary. One must reread Borges.

NATASHA WIMMER

CRIMES

She's sleeping with two men. She's had other lovers before and now she has two. That's the way it is. They don't know about each other. One says he's in love with her. The other one says nothing. She doesn't care much what either of them says. Declarations of love, declarations of hate. Words. She's sleeping with two men; that's just the way it is.

She's a journalist. Now she's sitting in a bar near the newspaper office with a book open in front of her, but she can't read. She tries, but she can't. She's distracted by what's happening outside, although there's nothing special to see. She shuts the book and stands up. The man behind the bar sees her coming and smiles. She asks what she owes him. The man names a sum. She opens her purse and hands him a note. How's things? asks the man. She looks him in the eye and says: So so. The man asks her if she'd like something more. On the house. She shakes her head, No, I'm fine, thanks. She stands there for a while, waiting for something. Then almost inaudibly she takes her leave and walks out of the bar.

She returns unhurriedly to the office. Waiting for the elevator, she notices a young man, about twenty-five, wearing an old suit and a tie whose design intrigues her: identical sky-blue faces screwed up in surprise against a background of watery green. Beside the young man, on the floor, is a suitcase of considerable dimensions. They say hello. The doors of the elevator open and both of them get in. Having examined her, the young man says that he sells socks, and that if she's interested he can offer her a good deal. She says she's not interested and then she thinks that it's strange to find a sock salesman inside the building, especially at a time when most of the offices are closed. The sock salesman gets out first, at the third floor, where there's an architect's studio and the office of a legal firm. As he's stepping out of the elevator, he raises his left hand and touches his forehead with the tips of his fingers. A salute, she thinks, and smiles at him. As the doors of the elevator close, he returns her smile.

When she gets back to the newspaper office, the only person there is a woman, sitting on a chair next to the window, smoking. The journalist goes to her desk, switches on her computer, and then walks over to the window. At this point the woman who's smoking realizes she's there and looks at her. The journalist sits on the windowsill and looks down into the street, which, unusually, makes her feel dizzy. Both of them are quiet for a few seconds. The woman who's smoking asks the journalist if she's OK. Fine, she says, I came back to finish the article about Calama. The smoking woman turns and looks out of the window at the river of cars flowing away from the city center, then half closes her eyes and laughs. I read something about it, she says. Complete shit, says the journalist. It was kind of funny, says the woman who's smoking. I don't get you, says the journalist. After thinking for a moment, the smoking woman says, Actually, it wasn't funny at all, and looks out of the window at the traffic again. Then the journalist gets up and walks over to her desk. She has stories to file and she's running late. She takes a walkman from a drawer and puts the headphones on. She gets to work. But after a while she takes the headphones off and turns on her chair. There's something weird about all this, she says. The woman who's smoking looks at her and asks her what she's talking about. About the woman in Calama, she says. At that moment the silence in the newspaper office is absolute. Or so it seems. Not even the hum of the elevator.

She was twenty-seven and she was stabbed twenty-seven times. Too much of a coincidence. Why? says the smoking woman, stuff like that happens. It's a lot of stab wounds, the journalist replies, but without much conviction. I've seen stranger things than that, says the woman who's smoking. After a moment of silence she adds: And maybe that's just a typo anyway. It could be, thinks the journalist. Is something bothering you? asks the smoking woman. The victim, the journalist replies. It could have been any of us. The woman who's smoking looks at her with a raised eyebrow. It could have been me, says the journalist. No way—you're nothing like her, says the smoking woman. I'm sleeping with two men like she was, says the journalist. The woman who's smoking smiles and repeats: No way. Everyone's against her, one way or another. Against who? The victim, of course. The smoking woman shrugs her shoulders. The reporters who cover stories like this are no better than the killers. Not all of them, says the woman who's smoking, there are some really good ones. Most of them are useless barflies, murmurs the journalist. Not all of them, says the smoking woman. Twenty-seven years old, twenty-seven stab wounds, I'm not convinced. Anyhow, they might have got the victim's age mixed up with the number of stab wounds. She had a nine-year-old kid, says the journalist, holding the headphones in her left hand and stroking them. The woman who's smoking stubs out the cigarette in the ashtray beside the window and stands up. Let's go, she says. No, I'm going to stay for a bit, says the journalist, and puts the headphones back on.

She's listening to Delalande. Her back is hurting, but otherwise she feels fine and she's keen to keep working. Out of the corner of her eye she watches the woman who was smoking lean over her desk and put something into her handbag. Soon she feels her colleague's hand gently pressing her shoulder to say good-bye. She goes on working. After half an hour she gets up and goes to the newspaper's archives (which are hardly ever consulted any more) and that's when she sees him.

He's standing there, just outside the open door, not daring to cross the threshold, looking at her with a half-smile on his face. She stifles a cry and asks him what he wants. It's me, he says, the sock salesman. The suitcase is sitting at his feet. I know, she says, I don't want to buy anything. I just wanted to have a little look around, he says. She examines him for a few seconds; she's not frightened now but angry, and she senses that the presence of the young salesman is a sign of something important, but what that something is eludes her grasp. All she knows is that it's important (or has some degree of importance) and that she's no longer afraid. Haven't you ever been in a newspaper office? she asks. I haven't, actually, he says. Come in, she says. He hesitates or pretends to hesitate and then he picks up the suitcase and walks in. Are you a journalist? She nods. And what are you writing? She tells him she's writing an article about a murder. The salesman puts the suitcase down again and his gaze wanders from table to table. Can I tell you something? She looks at him and her mind is blank. In the elevator, he says, it seemed to me that you were suffering for some reason. Me? she says. Yes, I thought you were suffering, although of course I don't know why. Everyone suffers, she says, as if they were talking in general terms. Neither of them has taken a seat. He's standing with his back to the door. She has retreated and is standing near the window. Both of them are frozen now, tensely upright, waiting. But when they speak, their voices have a false tone of familiarity.

What murder are you working on? he asks. The murder of a woman, she says. He smiles. He has a nice smile, she thinks, although it makes him look older (he's probably no more than twenty-five). It's always women who get killed, he says, and gestures with his right hand in a way that she can't interpret. As if she'd suddenly woken up, she realizes that she's alone in the office with a stranger, at a time when the building is almost empty. A slight shudder sweeps through her body. He notices, and looks for a place to sit down, as if to reassure her. Seated, he looks even taller than he is. Tell me about it, he says. The request exasperates her. Wait till the issue comes out. No, tell me now, maybe I can make a suggestion, he says. You're an expert on the subject, are you? she says. He looks at her without replying. She realizes she's made a mistake and tries to correct it, but before she can say anything more, he tells her that he's not an expert on murder. And why should I tell you about it? she says. Maybe you need to talk to someone. You could be right, she says. He smiles again. It was a woman who'd broken up with her husband, she says. Did the husband kill her? No. The husband has nothing to do with the crime. How come you're so sure? Because they arrested the killer the same day, she says. Ah, I see, he says. She was twenty-seven, she broke up with her husband, then she had a boyfriend, she lived with him, a younger guy, twenty-four, then she split with this boyfriend and starting going out with another guy. Boyfriend A and boyfriend B, he says. If you like, she says, and suddenly she feels calm, tired and calm, as if a part of the imaginary struggle (whose rules remain opaque to her) was already over and done.

I'm guessing, says the sock salesman, that this woman was good-looking. Yes, she was a beautiful woman, and very young too. Well, not all that young, he says. So you think a twenty-seven-year-old woman isn't young? Come on, let's be objective: young, sure, but not *very* young, he says. How old are you? Twenty-nine. I would have guessed twenty-five, she says. No, twenty-nine. He doesn't ask her age. Did she work or did she live off her boyfriends? She was a secretary. This woman never lived off anyone. And she had a nine-year-old son. And who killed her, boyfriend A or boyfriend B? he asks. Who would you say? Boyfriend A, of course. She nods. Because he was jealous. Yes, she says. But do you think it was just because he was jealous? No, she says. Ah, so you see, we have the same theory, you and I, he says. She chooses not to reply and moves away from the window. I should switch on a light, he says. No, leave it, she says, pulling out a chair and sitting down. After a while, he says: And it's getting you down, this story about a murder that happened a couple of months ago, I think it was. She looks at him and says nothing. Maybe you identify with the victim? Are you married? No, she says, but I've thought about her quite a bit. Are you married? No, me neither, he says, but I've lived with a few women. Do you think men have a problem with women who like sex? he asks. She looks away: beyond the windowpane night is enfolding the buildings. What she feels is a kind of claustrophobia. She got killed because she liked it, the journalist says without looking at him. She hears him say, Ah, and the tone of that ah is somewhere between irony and agony. She used to get up early, at a quarter past six every morning. She worked for a mining company in Calama, she was a secretary, and the stories in the papers say that her love life was a continual source of conflict. A continual source, he repeats, how poetic. Men kept falling in love with her, although she wasn't classically beautiful, she says. Beauty's relative, he says: There's a kind of beauty for everyone. Do you think? she asks, and looks at him again, steadily. Yes I do, says the sock salesman, everyone: the ugly, the not-so-ugly, the average-looking and the beautiful. But just because the not-so-ugly seem desirable to the ugly, that doesn't make them beautiful. So you get what I mean, he says. Yes, I get what you mean, she says ironically, but I don't agree; beauty's the same for everyone, like justice. Justice is the same for everyone? Don't make me laugh, he says. In theory, at least. It's all different in theory, he sighs, but let's not argue; tell me more about your murdered secretary. Did you see the body? The body? No, I didn't see it. I didn't cover the story, I just wrote an article about the crime. So you didn't go to the morgue in Calama? You didn't see the victim or talk with the killer? She looks at him and smiles mysteriously. The killer, yeah, I talked with him, she says.

Well, that's something, at least, he says. And? Nothing, she says, we talked, he told me he was sorry for what he'd done, he said he was crazy about the victim. Well put, he says. They met at the airport in Calama; he was a security guard, and she worked there for a while, as a receptionist. Before getting the job at the mine, says the sock salesman. In a mining company, she says. Same thing, he says. Well, not exactly. And how did he kill her? he asks. With a knife, she says. He stabbed her twenty-seven times. Don't you think that's strange? He looks down at the toes of his shoes for a few seconds. Then he looks at her again and says, What am I supposed to think is strange? The fact that she was twenty-seven and got stabbed twenty-seven times? Then a fury seizes her and she says, I'm in pretty much the same situation, so I guess I'm going to get killed one day too. She's on the point of saying, And you're the sad bastard who's going to kill me, but she checks herself just in time. She's shaking. But he can't tell from where he's sitting. To sum up: it's her ex who kills her. The night of the murder she sleeps with the current boyfriend. The ex knows what's going on. She's told him and he's been informed by others. Jealousy is eating him. He badgers and threatens her. But she pays him no attention; she's decided to get on with her life. She's met another man. They sleep together. That's the key to the crime: by refusing to give anything up she signs her death warrant. Yes, says the sock salesman, now I understand. No, you don't understand at all.

I CAN'T READ

This story is about four people. Two children, Lautaro and Pascual, a woman, Andrea, and another child, named Carlos. It's also about Chile, and, in a way, about Latin America in general.

When my son Lautaro was eight years old, he made friends with Pascual, who was four at the time. A friendship between children of such different ages is unusual, and maybe it was entirely due to the fact that when they met, in November 1998, Lautaro hadn't seen or played with another child for days on end, because Carolina and I had been trundling him around all over the place, much to his disgruntlement. It was Carolina's first trip to Chile and my first trip back since leaving in January 1974.

So when Lautaro met Pascual they immediately became friends.

I think it was when we went to have dinner with Pascual's

parents. The second time they met was when Alexandra, Pascual's mother, took Carolina and Lautaro to a swimming pool. I didn't go. And the boys might have seen each other again later on. So twice, or three times at the most.

The swimming pool was in the foothills of the Cordillera and, according to Carolina, the water was icy cold and neither she nor Alexandra went in. But Pascual and Lautaro did, and they had a great time.

A strange thing happened (one of the many strange things that will happen in this story and carry it and perhaps turn out to be what it's really about): when they got to the swimming pool, Lautaro asked Carolina if he could have a pee. She, of course, said yes, and then Lautaro went to the edge of the pool, pulled down his trunks a bit and peed into the water. That night, Carolina said that she'd been embarrassed, not for Lautaro, but because of what Alexandra might have thought. The fact is Lautaro had never done anything like that before. The swimming pool wasn't really busy, but there were a few people, and my son is not some wild boy who pees wherever he feels like it. It was very strange, Carolina said that night: the enormous Cordillera looming behind the swimming pool as if it were *waiting*, the laughter and the muted voices of the adults, oblivious to Lautaro's surprising urination, and Lautaro himself, wearing only his swimming trunks, peeing onto the blue surface of the water. What happened next? I asked. Well, she got up from where she was sunbathing, walked over to our son, and took him to the bathroom. It was like he was under hypnosis, said Carolina. Then he felt ashamed and didn't want to get into the pool, where Pascual was already splashing around, though after a while he forgot all about it and went in. But Carolina didn't. Alexandra asked if it was because of the pee, and Carolina said it was because of the cold, which was the truth.

I'd met Alexandra at the airport, a few minutes after stepping off the plane. It was almost a quarter of a century since I'd been in Chile. I'd been invited by *Paula* magazine, as one of the judges for their short story competition, and when we got through customs and immigration, Alexandra was there waiting for us, along with some people I didn't know. When she said her name, Alexandra Edwards, I asked her if she was the daughter of Jorge Edwards, the writer, and she looked at me, frowned slightly, as if considering how to reply, then said no. I'm the daughter of the photographer, she explained a little while later. By that stage I was already one of her admirers. I have to say it's not hard to admire her, because she's very pretty. But it wasn't her physical beauty that impressed me; it was something else, a side of her that I've gradually come to know and will probably never know completely, and yet I know it well enough to be sure that we'll always be friends. We'd arrived in the morning, and that afternoon, I remember, I had lunch with the rest of the judges, and I had to make a speech, and Alexandra was there, on the other side of the table, laughing with her eyes, which is something that Chilean women often do, or that's how it seemed to me at the time, a mistaken impression that must have been due to finding myself back in the country after so many years away; women everywhere laugh with their eyes, all the time, and men do too occasionally, and sometimes it's actually happening, and sometimes we only think it is, that silent laughter, which reminds me of Andrea, who is one of the main characters in this story, Andrea and Lautaro and Pascual and Carlitos, but I still hadn't met Andrea, or Pascual, and I'd never even heard of Carlitos, although the fortunate day was drawing near, as someone might have said—myself, perhaps, in January 1974.

Anyway, in spite of the age difference, Lautaro and Pascual became friends, and maybe it was there at the swimming pool perched in the foothills of the Cordillera that their friendship was cemented, after the peeing incident. When Carolina told me, I couldn't believe it: Lautaro urinating, not *in* the pool, underwater, as almost all kids do, but from the edge, for everyone to see.

That night, however, I fell asleep and dreamed of my son in that landscape, which had once been mine, the landscape of my twentieth year, and I came to understand a part of what he must have felt. If I'd been killed in Chile, at the end of 1973 or the beginning of 1974, he wouldn't have been born, I thought, and the act of urinating from the edge of the swimming pool—as if he were asleep or had suddenly been overtaken by a dream—was a physical way of acknowledging that fact and its shadow: having been born and being in a world that might have existed without him.

In the dream I understood that when Lautaro peed in the pool, he was dreaming too, and I understood that although I would never be able to approach his dream, I would always be there beside him. And when I woke up I remembered that one night, when I was a boy, I got out of bed and urinated abundantly in my sister's closet. But I was a sleepwalker, and Lautaro, fortunately, is not.

During that trip, which took up almost all of November 1998, I didn't see Andrea. Well, I did, but without really seeing her.

I met Alexandra and Alexandra's partner, Marcial, both of whom became friends, and whatever I say about them will be conditioned by the friendship that binds us, so perhaps it's better that I don't say too much.

But I didn't see Andrea. If I think back, all I can remember is a smile, like the smile of the Cheshire Cat, in the corridor of Alexandra and Marcial's apartment, a voice emerging from the shadows, a pair of dark and very deep eyes that were laughing as Alexandra's eyes had laughed when I made my first speech, just after arriving in Chile, but with a significant difference: Andrea, unlike Alexandra, was an invisible woman. I mean, she was invisible for me; at some point I saw her without really seeing her; I heard her, but I couldn't tell where her voice was coming from.

One of the things that Lautaro did around that time was to invent a method for approaching automatic doors without making them open. So in a way—I don't know if it was before or after our first trip to Chile (shortly before, I think)—he too began to play at being invisible, and quite successfully too.

The first time I saw him demonstrate this skill was in Blanes, at a bakery in Blanes, before that trip to Chile. I can't remember which writer said that if God was omnipresent, automatic doors should always be open. And since they're not, God doesn't exist. As well as being remarkable in itself, my son's method put paid to that argument. Lautaro didn't approach from the sides. Sometimes the sensors are placed in such a way that they don't register a sidelong approach and the doors remain closed. That's the easy or tricky way (though there's really not much of a trick to it), but my son chose the hard way; that is, he confronted the doors head on, refusing to stack the odds in his favor, adopting a direct approach, which the sensors are bound to detect and react to, opening the doors to let you in or out.

The originality of his technique lay in the movements that he made as he came toward the automatic doors. He would start off slowly, as if measuring the sensor's range, tapping his feet intermittently, as if the sensor could pick up vibrations in the ground, and moving his arms like the slowly turning sails of a windmill. Then the door would open, allowing him to gauge the critical distance. He would step back immediately and the door would close again, and then the real approach would begin. Each movement was slowed down as far as possible. His feet, for instance, didn't leave the ground; he slid them imperceptibly. His arms, held away from his torso, moved very slightly, like insects or auxiliary craft, as if unattached, as if this approach were being made not by a single body but by a shadow and two phantom shadows, two pilot shadows, and even his face was transformed; it seemed to blur but also to be concentrating on invisibility, on stasis and movement, on insubstantiality and paradox.

Once, in a big department store in Barcelona, I tried, in vain, to imitate him; the sensor kept detecting me, the doors opened every time. Lautaro, however, could go right up and touch the glass, reinforced or not, with the tip of his nose, unnoticed by the electronic eye, and this couldn't be explained, as I thought at first, by his height, because at eight my son was relatively tall, or by his slimness, since he's quite solidly built, but only by his aptitude, determination and skill.

Something else that I remember vividly from our first trip to Chile, and which enters unexpectedly into this story, is a bird. This bird was not invisible, but when it appeared one afternoon, I'm sure that I was the only one to see it.

We were staying in a serviced apartment in Providencia, on the eighth or the ninth story, and one afternoon when I had nothing to do I noticed a bird perched on one of the balconies of a neighboring building. For a while the bird sat still and seemed to be surveying the city as I was from the balcony of my apartment, except that the bird was looking at the city and I was looking at it. I'm myopic, my distance vision is poor, but at some point I reached the conclusion that this strange and solitary bird was a raptor, a falcon or something like that (I'm an ornithological ignoramus, except when it comes to parrots). Very soon after that, the falcon or whatever it was went plummeting down, which dispelled any doubts I might have still had. But then came the really surprising part: the bird began to fly toward my balcony. I was afraid but I didn't move.

It came to rest on the flat roof of a building right next to ours, and for a while we examined each other. Until I couldn't bear it any longer and went back inside.

The day this happened was also the day when Lautaro showed Pascual his knack of approaching automatic doors without making them open, and Pascual gave Lautaro an airplane. Lautaro loved the airplane; it had been one of Pascual's favorite toys, and maybe it was because of that gift that Lautaro showed him how to make like the invisible man, or, in Pascual's low-tech version, like an Indian.

I saw the boys from a café terrace where I was sitting with Alexandra, Carolina and Marcial. The others didn't see. I can't remember what we were talking about; all I remember is that Pascual and Lautaro approached a clothing store, unsuccessfully at first, because the door kept opening, and a woman with dyed blonde hair, wearing gray trousers and a black jacket, came out and said something to them, something I couldn't hear, partly because I was listening to what my wife and friends were saying, and partly because the store was a fair way off, on the far side of that covered square, and I remember Lautaro and Pascual running away at first, then I remember them standing, looking up, listening to that slim bottle blonde, who was probably telling them off, but then, when the woman disappeared back into the store, Lautaro resumed the operation while Pascual observed him from a predetermined spot, and at some point—I wasn't watching them all the time—my son succeeded in touching the glass of the closed door with his nose, and it was only then, two days before our flight back to Europe, that I knew I'd arrived in Chile and that everything would be all right. It was an apocalyptic thought.

In 1999, the following year, I went back to Chile at the invitation of the Book Fair. Almost all the Chilean writers decided to attack me *en patota*, as they say in Chile: that is, in a gang.

I guess it was their way of congratulating me for winning the Rómulo Gallegos Prize. I counterattacked. A woman of a certain age, who all her life had relied on the alms distributed to artists by a charitable state, called me a toady. Since I've never been a cultural attaché or held a sinecure, I was surprised by this accusation. I was also called a *patero*, which is not the same as a *patota*. A *patero* doesn't necessarily belong to a *patota*, as you might be forgiven for supposing, although there are always *pateros* in a *patota*. A *patero* is a sycophant, a flatterer, a brownnose, an asslicker. The amazing thing about these accusations is that they were made by left- as well as right-wing Chileans who were busy licking ass nonstop to hang onto their scraps of fame, while everything that I'd accomplished (not that it amounts to much) was down to me and no one else. What was it that they didn't like about me? Well, someone said it was my teeth. Fair enough; I can't argue with that.

BEACH

I gave up heroin and went home and began the methadone treatment administered at the outpatient clinic and I didn't have much else to do except get up each morning and watch TV and try to sleep at night, but I couldn't, something made me unable to close my eyes and rest, and that was my routine until one day I couldn't stand it anymore and I bought myself a pair of black swim trunks at a store in the center of town and I went to the beach, wearing the trunks and with a towel and a magazine, and I spread my towel not too far from the sea and then I lay down and spent a while trying to decide whether to go into the sea or not, I could think of lots of reasons to go in but also some not to (the children playing at the water's edge, for example), until at last it was too late and I went home, and the next morning I bought some sunscreen and I went to the beach again, and at around twelve I headed to the clinic and got my dose of methadone and said hello to some familiar faces, no friends, just familiar faces from the methadone line who were surprised to see me in swim trunks, but I acted as if there was nothing strange about it, and then I walked back to the beach and this time I went for a dip and tried to swim, though I couldn't, and that was enough for me, and the next day I went back to the beach and put on sunscreen all over and then I fell asleep on the sand, and when I woke up I felt very well-rested, and I hadn't burned my back or anything, and this went on for a week or maybe two, I can't remember, the only thing I'm sure of is that each day I got more tan and though I didn't talk to anyone each day I felt better, or different, which isn't the same thing but in my case it seemed like it, and one day an old couple turned up on the beach, I remember it clearly, it looked like they'd been together for a long time, she was fat, or round, and must have been about seventy, and he was thin, or more than thin, a walking skeleton, I think that was why I noticed him, because usually I didn't take much notice of the people on the beach, but I did notice them, and it was because the guy was so skinny, I saw him and got scared, fuck, it's death coming for me, I thought, but nothing was coming for me, it was just two old people, the man maybe seventy-five and the woman about seventy, or the other way around, and she seemed to be in good health, but he looked as if he were going to breathe his last breath any time now or as if this were his last summer, and at first, once I was over my initial fright, it was hard for me to look away from the old man's face, from his skull barely covered by a thin layer of skin, but then I got used to watching the two of them surreptitiously, lying on the sand, on my stomach, with my face hidden in my arms, or from the boardwalk, sitting on a bench facing the beach, as I pretended to brush sand off myself, and I remember that the old woman always came to the beach with an umbrella, under which she quickly ducked, and she didn't wear a swimsuit, although sometimes I saw her in a swimsuit, but usually she was in a very loose summer dress that made her look fatter than she was, and under that umbrella the old woman sat reading, she had a very thick book, while the skeleton that was her husband lay on the sand in nothing but a tiny swimsuit, almost a thong, and drank in the sun with a voracity that brought me distant memories of junkies frozen in blissful immobility, of junkies focused on what they were doing, on the only thing they could do, and then my head ached and I left the beach, I had something to eat on the Paseo Marítimo, a little dish of anchovies and a beer, and then I smoked a cigarette and watched the beach through the window of the bar, and then I went back and the old man and the old woman were still there, she under her umbrella, he exposed to the sun's rays, and then, suddenly, for no reason, I felt like crying and I got in the water and swam and when I was a long way from the shore I looked at the sun and it seemed strange to me that it was there, that big thing so unlike us, and then I started to swim toward the beach (twice I almost drowned) and when I got back I dropped down next to my towel and sat there panting for quite a while, but without losing sight of the old couple, and then I may have fallen asleep on the sand, and when I woke up the beach was beginning to empty, but the old man and the old woman were still there, she with her novel under the umbrella and he on his back in the sun with his eyes closed and a strange expression on his skull-like face, as if he could feel each second passing and he was savoring it, though the sun's rays were weak, though the sun had already dipped behind the buildings along the beach, behind the hills, but that didn't seem to bother him, and then I watched him and I watched the sun, and sometimes my back stung a little, as if that afternoon I'd burned myself, and I looked at them and then I got up, I slung my towel over my shoulders like a cape and went to sit on one of the benches of the Paseo Marítimo, where I pretended to brush nonexistent sand off my legs, and from up there I had a different vision of the couple, and I said to myself that maybe he wasn't about to die, I said to myself that maybe time didn't exist in the way I'd always thought it existed, I reflected on time as the sun's distance lengthened the shadows of the buildings, and then I went home and took a shower and examined my red back, a back that didn't seem to belong to me but to someone else, someone I wouldn't get to know for years and then I turned on the TV and watched shows that I didn't understand at all, until I fell asleep in my chair, and the next day it was back to the same old thing, the beach, the clinic, the beach again, a routine that was sometimes interrupted by new people on the beach, a woman, for example, who was always standing, who never lay down in the sand, who wore a bikini bottom and a blue T-shirt, and who only went into the water up to the knees, and who was reading a book, like the old woman, but this woman read it standing up, and sometimes she knelt down, though in a very odd way, and picked up a big bottle of Pepsi and drank, standing up, of course, and then put the bottle back down on the towel, which I don't know why she'd brought since she never lay down on it or went swimming, and sometimes this woman scared me, she seemed too strange, but most of the time I just felt sorry for her, and I saw other strange things too, all kinds of things happen at the beach, maybe because it's the only place where we're all half-naked, though nothing too important ever happened, once as I was walking along the shore I thought I saw an ex-junkie like me, sitting on a mound of sand with a baby on his lap, and another time I saw some Russian girls, three Russian girls, who were probably hookers and who were talking on cell phones and laughing, all three of them, but what really interested me most was the old couple, partly because I had the feeling that the old man might die at any moment, and when I thought this, or when I realized I was thinking this, crazy ideas would come into my head, like the thought that after the old man's death there would be a tsunami and the town would be destroyed by a giant wave, or that the earth would begin to shake and a massive earthquake would swallow up the whole town in a wave of dust, and when I thought about all this, I hid my head in my hands and began to weep, and while I was weeping I dreamed (or imagined) that it was nighttime, say three in the morning, and I'd left my house and gone to the beach, and on the beach I found the old man lying on the sand, and in the sky, up near the stars, but closer to Earth than the other stars, there shone a black sun, an enormous sun, silent and black, and I went down to the beach and lay on the sand too, the only two people on the beach were the old man and me, and when I opened my eyes again I realized that the Russian hookers and the girl who was always standing and the ex-junkie with the baby were watching me curiously, maybe wondering who that weird guy was, the guy with the sunburned shoulders and back, and even the old woman was gazing at me from under her umbrella, interrupting the reading of her interminable book for a few seconds, maybe wondering who that young man was, that man with silent tears running down his face, a man of thirty-five who had nothing at all but who was recovering his will and his courage and who knew that he would live a while longer.

NATASHA WIMMER

MUSCLES

1.

I don't know if my brother was a cultured or civilized person, though some nights I think that he probably was and that being civilized is probably what saved him from suicide.

His favorite books were *Kabyle Customs* by John Hodge and all the volumes of Professor Ramiro Lira's *Works of the Pre-Socratic Philosophers* (which are more like pamphlets, really, but my brother explained that this was because the works of those poor philosophers had been swallowed by the black hole of time, which is what will happen to all of us). And others.

"No hole's going to swallow me," I'd say to him.

"It's going to happen to both of us, Marta, there's no avoiding it," he'd say, without a hint of sadness.

But I think it's a very sad thought.

It was usually over breakfast that we talked about the Pre-Socratic philosophers. The one he liked best was Empedocles. That Empedocles, he used to say, he's like Spiderman. My favorite was Heraclitus. We almost never talked about the philosophers at night, I don't know why. It must have been because at night we had much more to talk about, or because sometimes we were both too tired when we got back from work—you need to be sharp if you're going to talk about philosophy—though little by little, and especially after the death of our parents, that began to change as well, and our nighttime conversations gradually became more grown-up; we started talking more seriously, as if our words were venturing into much more open and hazardous territory, now that our parents were no longer there to anchor them. But in the mornings, both before their death and after, our favorite topic was the Pre-Socratics, as if the start of a new day (though, if you think about it, the day begins long before that, at midnight) had restored the energy we had as kids and made everything different, better, refreshed. I remember our breakfasts: a cup of coffee with milk, bread with tomato and olive oil, a steak, a bowl of cereal or two tubs of yogurt with honey and muesli, Super Egg (100% egg protein), Fuel Tank (with megacalorie protein: 3000 calories per dose), Super Mega Mass, Victory Mega Aminos (in capsules), Fat Burner (lipotropes to help dissolve fat), and an orange, a banana or an apple, depending on the season. That was for Enric. I don't eat much: I'd have maybe half a biscuit, the kind my brother used to buy, made with whole wheat flour and enriched with some kind of vitamins, and a cup of black coffee.

There could be something invigorating about that table, seen from the kitchen, at seven-thirty or eight in the morning. The plates and the mugs and the bowls and the packets that looked like NASA rations seemed to be saying: "Go out into the street. The day is full of promise. The world is young and so are you." My brother would sit at that table and open a pamphlet containing the complete works of some Pre-Socratic philosopher, or a magazine, and while his right hand was busy with a spoon or a fork, his left hand would turn the pages.

"Listen to what this son of a bitch Diogenes of Apollonia says."

I'd keep quiet and wait for him to speak, doing my best to look attentive.

"'When beginning any account, it seems to me that one should make the starting point incontrovertible and the style simple and dignified.' How do you like that?"

"It sounds reasonable."

"It's fucking *reasonable* all right!"

After breakfast my brother helped me to take the dishes to the kitchen and then he went to work. From the age of sixteen he'd been working at Fonollosa Brothers Auto Repairs, near Plaza Molina, in a neighborhood where people have expensive, complicated cars to fix. I'd stay home a while longer, watching TV or reading one of the Pre-Socratics (we did the dishes at night) and then I'd go to work, that is to the Academía Malú; the name makes it sound like a school (a school for whores, my brother used to say), though in fact it's a hairdressing salon.

Why was my brother so rude about the Academía Malú? The answer's simple but it's a sore point. My friend or ex-friend Montse García worked there; Enric went out with her for a month or so, two at the most, till Montse decided that they weren't right for each other. At least that's how she explained it to me when they split up. My brother just mumbled something incomprehensible and from then on, whenever the Academía came up, he always made some snide or obscene remark.

"But what happened with you and Montse?" I asked him one night.

"Nothing," said my brother. "We were incompatible. It's none of your business."

My brother was like that, and the death of our parents just made it worse. Sometimes, from my room, I could hear him talking to himself: We're orphans, that's an irrefutable fact, and we have to get used it, he'd say. And then he'd repeat it, over and over, obsessively, like someone who's forgotten the real words to a song: We're orphans, we're orphans, etc. At times like that I wanted to hug him, or get up and take him a mug of hot milk, but that would've only made it worse; my brother would've broken down crying for sure, and after a while I'd have started crying too. So I never got out of bed, and he'd go on talking to himself until he was finally overtaken by sleep.

But in the morning I'd sometimes try to reason with him: "We're not the only orphans in the world. And anyway, to be an orphan, I mean a real orphan, I think you have to be a minor, and we're not minors any more."

"You are, Marta," he'd say, "and it's my duty to look after you."

According to Montse García, my brother was immature. I only went out with them twice when they were together, both times because my brother asked me to, and on both occasions I was able to confirm the accuracy of my friend's or ex-friend's judgment. The first time we went to see a movie by Almodóvar. Enric suggested a Van Damme movie, but Montse and I refused. We were late because of the argument, and when we arrived the cinema was dark, the film had started, and my brother decided, absurdly, not to sit with us. The second time we went to the gym, the Rosales gym in Calle Bonaventura, right near our place, where my brother works out every day. It wasn't that he didn't make an effort; this time, he was trying too hard. He wanted us to see him inserted into all the gym's contraptions, and in the end one of them nearly decapitated him. I'm fond of my brother, but there are limits, like the doors of the Rosales gym. I've never been able to stand bodybuilders; my idea of handsome may keep shifting unreliably, as my brother says, but it has never taken the form of a hulk. I should say that Montse García was with me on this, although at the time she was interested in my brother, and he'd been bodybuilding since he was sixteen (he started just after he got the job at the auto repair shop). I think it was one of the guys from his work, by the name of Paco Contreras, who got him into it. This Paco competed in various bodybuilding championships in Catalonia and then he moved to Dos Hermanas in Andalusia, where he died. Sometimes my brother would get a letter from him and read one or two sentences to me. Then he'd put the letters in a little chest that he kept under his bed, the only place in the house where things could be kept under lock and key. According to Montse, this Paco had perverted my brother. I told her the story myself and regretted it immediately. My brother may be many things but he isn't stupid, and certainly not simple (who is, really?), and yet the story, the way I told it, badly or partially, did made him look stupid. I never met Paco Contreras. According to my brother, he was an amazing guy, the best friend he'd ever have, etc., etc. So when Montse said that this Paco had perverted my brother, I told her she was wrong, Enric was a serious, responsible, clean-living person, the best brother I'd ever have.

"Well, what else could you say, you poor thing?"

Sometimes I wanted to kill her. But I did everything I could to make things work out between her and Enric. I preferred them to go out on their own, of course, though if it had been up to my brother, I've have gone along every time. A week after they started going out, Montse and I went to the bathroom at the Academía Malú and she asked me if my brother was sick.

"He's super-fit," I said.

"Well, something's not right," she said, and declined to elaborate, although I knew what she was referring to.

This happened a few months after the death of our parents. Montse was the first girl my brother had been out with. And there haven't been any others since. Sometimes I think that he must have been feeling alone and a bit lost in the world. Our parents died in a bus accident, on the way from Barcelona to Benidorm, setting off for their first vacation on their own. My brother was very close to them. So was I, but in a different way. The official who met us at the morgue in Benidorm (he was dressed like a pathologist, though I don't think he actually was one) told us that our parents' bodies had been found holding hands, and that it had been quite a job to separate them.

"It made an impression on us all, and I thought you'd like to know," he said.

"They must have been asleep at the time of the crash," said my brother. "They liked to sleep holding hands."

"And how do you know that?" I asked.

"It's the kind of thing an older brother knows," said the official or the pathologist.

"I saw them, lots of times," said my brother with tears brimming in his eyes.

Later, when we were in the hospital cafeteria, waiting for the papers so we could take our parents back to Barcelona, he said that it was all because of the calcination. He said that the crash must have caused an explosion, and the explosion would have produced a fireball hot enough to fuse the hands of our deceased progenitors.

"They would have had to use a saw to separate them."

He said this in a cold, offhand way, but I knew that my brother was suffering as he had never suffered before. So when he started going out with Montse García a few months later, I think one night I even prayed that he'd sleep with her and that they'd form some kind of lasting relationship. But what happened is that Montse, who had seemed keen before she went out with him, gradually cooled off and then she got bitter, and by the time they broke up sixty days later, she was treating me as an enemy, as if I were to blame for the disappointments of her short-lived romance. When she finally decided to break it off, our relationship improved markedly for a few days, and I even thought that we could go back to being good friends like before. But Enric's shadow kept coming between us whenever I tried to get close to her again.

"It can't be healthy to spend all day at the gym. Why would a guy want muscles like that, anyway? It isn't normal," she said to me one day.

"He also reads the Pre-Socratic philosophers," I replied.

"Like I said, your brother's not right in the head. You be careful. One night you might find him in your room with a knife, about to cut your throat."

"My brother is a kind person; he wouldn't hurt anyone."

"You're an idiot, Marta," she said, and that was the end of our friendship.

From then on, we only spoke to each other when it was strictly necessary for work: Pass me some clips, can I have the dryer, can you get that color down?

What a pity.

II.

One night my brother turned up with Tomé and Florencio. He'd never invited anyone home: not when our parents were alive, and not in the months since they died. At first I thought they were two friends from the gym but I only had to take a second look to realize that these guys didn't work out.

"They'll be staying here tonight," my brother said in the kitchen. We were getting dinner ready, and Florencio and Tomé were channel-surfing in the living room.

"Where?" I said. It's a small flat, and there's no guest room.

"In Mom and Dad's bedroom," he said, looking away.

He must have been expecting me to protest, but I thought it was a good idea, though maybe I was a bit surprised that I hadn't come up with it myself. Of course: our parents' empty bedroom. That was fine by me. I asked him who they were, where he'd met them, what they did.

"At the gym. They're South Americans."

We had salad and grilled steak for dinner.

Florencio and Tomé looked like they were nearly thirty, but I knew they'd look like that until they were fifty. They were hungry and they sampled every concoction my brother laid out on the table. I don't know if they were aware of the immense honor he was doing them, putting his stock of supplements at their disposal. I asked them if they were bodybuilders too.

"We do fitness training," said Tomé.

"Do you know what that is?" asked Florencio.

I don't like people thinking I'm stupid. Or ignorant, which is worse.

"Of course I know what it is; my brother's been going to the gym since he was sixteen," I said, and immediately wished I'd kept my mouth shut.

Florencio and Tomé laughed in unison, and then my brother laughed as well. I asked them what was so funny. My brother looked at me, lost for words, with an expression of utter bewilderment, but also of happiness, on his face.

"Feisty, aren't you?" said Florencio.

"Very feisty," said Tomé.

"She's always had a strong character, my sister," said Enric.

"And you've worked all this out from what I said about fitness training?"

"From the way you said it. Looking me in the eye. Sure of yourself," said Florencio.

"If I had my tarot pack here, I'd do a reading for you," said Tomé.

"So you do fitness training and tarot readings?"

"And a few other things as well," said Tomé.

Florencio and my brother laughed again. But in my brother's case it was, I realized, nervous rather than happy laughter. He was worried, although he was trying to hide it. The two South Americans, however, seemed relaxed, as if they were used to sleeping in a different house every night.

I finished eating before they did and went off to my bedroom and shut the door. My brother came to tell me there was a good movie on, but I said I had to get up early. I wasn't sleepy. I took off my shoes and flopped onto the bed, still dressed, with the complete works of Xenophanes of Colophon ("For all things are from earth and in earth all things end"), until I heard them get up from the table. First they went to the kitchen, washed the dishes, laughed again (what was there in the kitchen that could have made them laugh?) and then they came back to the living room and started watching something on TV. I can't remember falling asleep. But I do remember this: a sentence from Xenophanes ("He sees as a whole, he thinks as a whole, he hears as a whole") which for some reason I found unsettling. I was woken by noises from my brother's room. At first, although the light was still on in my room, I didn't know where I was. Then I heard the shouting and the moaning. It was my brother moaning, I was absolutely sure of that. And one of the South Americans was shouting (in an urgent, imperious, affectionate way), but I couldn't tell which one of them it was. I got undressed, put on my nightie, and for a while I just lay there listening and thinking. I tried to read Xenophanes, but I couldn't get past the following sentence or fragment: "wild cherry." It made me feel very sad. Then I got up and tried to hear what the South American was saying. With my ear to the wall I could hear the odd word or sentence (in a way it was like reading the fragments of Xenophanes): "that's the way," "nice and tight," "careful," "slowly." Then I went back to bed and fell asleep. In the morning, for the first time in I don't know how many years, my brother didn't have breakfast with me.

I thought they'd done something to him; I knocked on his door. After a while he said to come in. The room smelt of the hair-removal cream my brother uses. I asked him if he was sick. He said no, he was fine, but he thought he'd go to work a bit later.

"And the South Americans?"

"In Mom and Dad's room, sleeping. We stayed up late last night."

"I heard you," I said. "You went to bed with one of them."

My brother surprised me by laughing.

"Did we wake you up?"

"No, I woke up anyway, I was feeling restless, then I heard you. By chance. I wasn't spying on you."

"Well, it's no big deal. Let me get a bit more sleep."

I stood there, frozen, watching him, not knowing what to do or say, until I heard voices in Mom and Dad's room and then I turned around and walked out of the apartment without having breakfast. I worked all morning in a daze, as if I was the one who hadn't gotten any sleep. At midday I went to have lunch at a Chinese restaurant where some of the other girls from the Academía Malú used to go and then I went walking in the streets around Plaza de España. I thought about when I was seven and my brother was sixteen and he was the person I loved most in the world. One time he told me that his dream was to play Maciste when he grew up. I had no idea who Maciste was, so he showed me a picture of him in a movie magazine. I didn't like him. You're much better looking, I said, and he looked pleased and smiled. Then, for some reason, as I was walking around, I remembered him hugging Mom and Dad, giving them all his pay, taking me to the movies (though we never went to see a Maciste film), and doing little poses in front of the mirror in the elevator.

I must have been feeling terrible that afternoon—though I can't really remember; I know I was thinking about my brother and our apartment, and my mental images of him and of it seemed to be shackled, sunken, black and white, irreparable—and it must have been obvious because even Montse García came over to ask if there was something wrong.

"What could possibly be wrong?" I said. I guess I must have said it in a way that sounded aggressive, although I didn't mean to.

"Maybe that brother of yours has been horrible to you," said Montse.

"Enric is going through a rough patch, but he's gradually getting it together," I replied. "He's trying to find his way, which is more than you can say for some."

From the way Montse looked at me I guessed that she still felt something for him.

"Your brother's a bad person, seriously," she said. "He's never satisfied with anything, but he doesn't know what he wants. He'll screw things up for everyone else just to make himself happy, but the thing is he doesn't know how to be happy. Am I making myself clear?"

"I could kill you sometimes," I said.

"I know it's not easy to hear this stuff. But you're alone in the world, Marta, and you have to watch out for yourself. I like you. You're a good person and that's why I'm saying this, although I know you're not going to listen."

For a moment I was tempted to tell her about what had happened the night before, but I decided that it was better to keep my mouth shut.

That night, when I got home, Enric, Florencio and Tomé were already in the living room watching TV. I made a coffee and sat as far away from them as I could, at the end of the table, near the window, where my father used to sit. Enric and Tomé were sprawled on the sofa and Florencio was in the armchair, which is where I normally sit to watch TV. There were containers of high-calorie, high-protein food scattered over the table, the kind my brother eats, but these were new. I also saw a baguette, ham, cheese, and several bottles of beer.

"The guys brought some supplies," said my brother.

I didn't respond. The containers of food, the pills, the Fuel Tank and the Super Egg (vanilla and chocolate flavored, respectively) were expensive, more than five thousand pesetas a tub, and I couldn't imagine that scruffy pair having so much money. It would have cost them more than fifty thousand pesetas all together.

"Where did you steal it from?"

"I like your sister," said Florencio.

My brother looked at me and then at them with a half-amused, half-incredulous expression on his face.

"We went to get some stuff from our place," said Florencio. "And we decided to pick up some food on the way."

"I brought my tarot cards as well," said Tomé.

"If you have a place of your own, why do you want to move in here?"

"That was just a manner of speaking," said Florencio. "Actually, it's a boarding house. When you don't have a place of your own, you end up calling any place home, even a shithole like that boarding house. Enric invited us to stay here for a few days, till we see how things work out."

"In other words, you're broke."

"You could say our finances are tight."

At that moment, for some reason, they looked handsome to me. Both of them had just taken a shower. Tomé's hair was still wet, and his manner was unassuming but self-assured.

Everything seemed to be much simpler and clearer for them than it was for my brother and me.

"So you stole that food."

"Well, yeah, that's right, we did," said Florencio.

"We thought it would be rude to turn up empty-handed, and Enric likes that stuff; he spends a fortune on it."

"It isn't cheap, that's for sure," said my brother.

"We went to a store on Avenida Roma, near the Modelo Prison, a store that specializes in bodybuilding supplements, and we took whatever we could."

"You shouldn't have done that, guys," my brother said.

"Hey, it was the least we could do," said Tomé.

My brother smiled happily: "Now I have supplies for like five months."

"What if you'd been caught?" I said.

"We never get caught," said Florencio.

"We bought a packet of soy cookies," said Tomé.

Suddenly I ran out of arguments. I would have liked to ask them how many days they were planning to stay at our place, but I didn't want to go too far. It's one thing to be frank and another to be rude. It's one thing to be aggressive and another to be hospitable. So I kept quiet, sitting on my father's chair, staring at the bottom of my coffee cup and occasionally glancing up at the game show they were watching on TV (Florencio and Tomé knew all the answers) until it was time to eat.

"The guys made dinner tonight," said my brother.

Poor fool, I thought, without getting up. That night we ate rice and vegetables. My brother, who always eats meat, didn't complain; on the contrary, he praised the flavor of the meal and went back for seconds and thirds. Florencio set the table, and Tomé served the food. They opened a bottle of expensive wine ("You stole this too?" I asked—"Naturally," replied Florencio) and we all had some.

"Let's drink a toast to Marta and Enric," said Tomé. "Two very special people. There's no else like you two."

I could feel myself blushing. I'm not used to drinking wine (my parents were teetotalers, my brother too, until yesterday, anyway) and I'm even less used to public compliments.

TRANSLATOR'S NOTE: The quotations from Diogenes of Apollonia and Xenophanes of Colophon in "Muscles" are given in Jonathan Barnes's translation, from *Early Greek Philosophy* (London: Penguin, 1987).

THE TOUR

My idea was to interview John Malone, the musician who'd disappeared. Five years earlier, Malone had already slipped out of the dark zone where the legends live, and he wasn't really newsworthy any more, although the fans hadn't forgotten his name. In the seventh decade of the twentieth century, along with Jacob Morley and Dan Endycott, he'd been a founding member of Broken Zoo, one of the most successful rock groups of the time. Broken Zoo recorded their first LP in 1966. It was a magnificent record, up there with the best stuff coming out of England—and this is the mid-sixties I'm talking about, with the Beatles and the Rolling Stones in top form. The second LP came out soon after and, to everyone's surprise, it was even better than the first. Broken Zoo did a tour of Europe and then a tour of the States. The North American tour went on for months. As they traveled from city to city, the record climbed up the charts and finally reached number one. When they got back to London, they took a few days off to rest. Morley shut himself up in a house that he'd recently bought on the outskirts of London, where he had a private recording studio. Endycott kept himself busy getting off with all the pretty groupies who came swarming around the band, till one of them got off with him, and they bought a house in Belgravia and got married. As for Malone, he seemed more lethargic. According to some of the books about Broken Zoo, he attended "weird parties," though what the authors meant by *weird* is not exactly clear. I'm guessing it's what they said back then to indicate a mix of sex and drugs. Shortly afterward, Malone disappeared. And after sensibly allowing a month or two to elapse, Broken Zoo's manager called a press conference, at which he admitted what everyone already knew: John Malone had quit the group without a word of explanation. Not long after that, Morley and Endycott, along with the drummer Ronnie Palmer, and another band member called Corrigan, came out with their own versions of the events. Malone hadn't been in touch with anyone except Palmer. He called him three weeks after his disappearance, just to say that he was fine, and to tell them not to wait for him because he wasn't planning to come back. Many people thought that this would be the end of the group. Malone was the best of the lot, and it was hard to imagine Broken Zoo going on without him. But then Morley shut himself up for a month or so in his mansion, and Endycott went there too and worked ten hours a day, and they put together the group's third LP. Contrary to the expectations of the critics, Broken Zoo's third record was better than the first and the second. Seventy percent of the material on the first record was written by Malone: lyrics as well as music. On the second record, it was seventy-five percent. The rest was provided by Morley and Endycott, except for one track, which is something of an anomaly, with lyrics co-written by Morley and Palmer. For the third record, however, Morley and Endycott wrote ninety percent of the material, and the remaining ten percent was contributed by Palmer, Morley, Endycott and a new member, Venable, who'd joined the group when it was clear that Malone wouldn't be coming back. One of the songs is dedicated to Malone. There's no bitterness in it. Just friendship and admiration. The title is "When are You Going to Come Back?" It was released as a single and in less than two weeks it went to the top of the charts in London. Malone, of course, didn't come back, and although, at the time, various journalists went searching for him, all their efforts were fruitless. There was even a rumor that he had died in a city in France and been buried in a pauper's grave. Broken Zoo's third album was followed by a fourth, which was greeted with unanimous praise, and after the fourth came a fifth and then a sixth, a flawless double album, the group's apotheosis, and after that they didn't play for while, but then they brought out a seventh LP, which was pretty good, and then an eighth, and in the middle of the eighties they made their ninth album, another double, and Morley and Endycott must have signed a pact with the devil, because this record swept the world, from Japan to Holland, from New Zealand to Canada, tearing through Thailand like a tornado, which is really saying something. Then the group broke up, though every now and then, on a special occasion, they'd get back together to play their old songs at a select venue. In 1995 a journalist from *Rolling Stone* found out where Malone was living. His article stunned the die-hard fans of Broken Zoo, who cherished the group's first vinyl LPs. But most of the magazine's readers didn't really care what had happened to a guy who was widely assumed to be dead. In a way, Malone's life during all those years had been a living death. When he left London, he had simply gone back to his parents' house. That was all. He stayed there for two years, doing nothing, while the members of his old band set out to take the universe by storm.

DANIELA

My name is Daniela de Montecristo and I am a citizen of the universe, although I was born in Buenos Aires, the capital of Argentina, in the year 1915, the youngest of three sisters. Later my father remarried and had a little son, but the child died before his first birthday, and Papa had to be happy with what he had, that is, with my sisters and me. I don't know why I'm explaining all this. It's ancient history, or children's stories if you like, of no interest to anyone now. I lost my virginity at the age of thirteen. That might interest someone. I was deflowered by one of the ranch hands. I can't remember his name, all I know is that he was a ranch hand and must have been somewhere between twenty-five and forty-five. He didn't rape me, I do remember that. At least I never thought of it as rape, afterward I mean, when it was over, and I was getting dressed behind an ombu tree, and the ranch hand, around the other side, was pensively rolling a cigarette, which he then lit and gave me for a couple of puffs on it, my first ever puffs of smoke. I remember that vividly. The bitter taste of the tobacco and the plains stretching away endlessly and my legs trembling. What was really trembling, though, were my thoughts. I could have gone and told on him. All that night I kept turning the idea over in my mind, and the next two nights as well. But I didn't do it. Partly because I wanted to repeat the experience. Partly because it wasn't my father's ranch; it belonged to one of his friends, so the punishment wouldn't have been administered by my blood relations, it would have fallen outside what I took to be the ambit of real justice, the justice of the blood. My father never had a ranch. My older sister married a lawyer, a pathetic shyster who never tired of declaring his inordinate love for my father. My other sister married the son of a ranch owner, a crazy kid who within a few years managed to gamble away a small fortune and get himself cut out of the will. To sum up: my family was always middle class, and whatever efforts we made, from our various starting points, in our various and often contradictory ways, to climb up a rung and enter the rigid, immutable upper crust, official guardian of justice and morality, the fact is we never moved out of our social compartment, which, although comfortable, condemned the livelier minds in the clan (myself, for example) to a restlessness that even then, at the age of thirteen, on that ranch, which wasn't our property, I could glimpse like a dizzying mirage, a space in time where time itself was cancelled, time as we know it, and that was why I began by saying that I am a citizen of the universe and not, as the saying goes, of the world, because I may be old but it should be quite clear that I'm not stupid, and the world cannot contain a dizzying mirage like that, although perhaps the universe can. But I was talking about restlessness. I was talking about the night when I thought about telling on the ranch hand who had deflowered me. I didn't, and I didn't have sex with him again. Restlessness, my first apprehension of restlessness, declared itself as a fever, so my father sent me back to Buenos Aires, where I was entrusted to the care of a physician, Dr. Guarini.

SUNTAN

The previous summer I'd been a temporary foster parent to a child from the Third World. It was a terrible experience. When I took her to the airport I was a wreck, and Olga (that was her name), she was a wreck as well. We cried all the way, we didn't stop for a minute. She kept sobbing that she wanted to stay with me, the poor thing. Just as well there were no photographers. Even so, I stayed in the car for a while, fixing my makeup, before we got out. The man from the NGO who was there to take the children back was waiting by the information counter. He looked at me and realized right away that I was taking it hard. It's normal, the first time, he said. There was another girl there with her foster family. In spite of the dark glasses, they recognized me immediately. The mother came over and said: It gives us such a boost to know that you're taking part in the program too, Lucía. I had no idea what she meant, but I smiled and said I was just another volunteer.

Half an hour later the children and the man from the NGO boarded the plane and disappeared, leaving the foster parents in the departure lounge. One of them suggested that we go for a drink. I declined. I shook hands with all of them (no kisses) and left. In the car I cried all the way back to my apartment, but two days later I had to go to Milan, for work, and I spent August in Marbella and Mallorca. Eventually the summer came to an end and work began again in earnest.

And all sorts of things happened after that.

Eight months later the same NGO wrote to me to see if I wanted to foster a child again in July. I thought about it all that day, carrying the letter around in my handbag, and eventually decided to repeat the experience. I called them and said I'd participate again, as long as they did whatever they could to make sure it was Olga. They said they'd try, but the organization had a rule, or something—I didn't understand. Call me, I said. A month later they called and said they were doing their best to get Olga. At that time I was acting in a play, a wonderful English production, a musical about the poor people of London, or maybe it was Manchester, set at the beginning of the century, a play in which I had to sing and dance as well as act. For some reason, talking with the people from the NGO helped me with my work. It was just after the première and the reviews hadn't been very good. Especially the comments about me. Well, not just me; some of the other actors came off badly too. After that phone call my performances improved; they were stronger, more convincing, and the others were inspired by my energy on stage.

Then I was offered a television show. I said yes without a second thought.

Then I met a doctor in Madrid called Gorka (his family came from the Basque country) and we fell in love.

To be completely honest, for a while I forgot all about the

girl and the NGO. I was living at a frantic pace: interviews, TV appearances, a small but gratifying part in a film, and my own talk show with celebrity guests (actresses, models, athletes, heartthrobs).

One morning they called and said that Olga wouldn't be able to spend her vacation month with me. Why not? I asked, although for a moment I had no idea who Olga was, what vacation month they were talking about, or who had called to tell me this and was now replying to my question in a condescending tone of voice that I didn't like at all, explaining something about regulations, which left me even more confused. When I finally realized what it was about, I said I didn't have time to talk right then and told them to call me back the following night, insisting that I wanted Olga. We completely understand, said the voice: It's human, it's normal.

Having reached this point in my story, there's something I think I should clarify. There are show-business personalities who'll stop at nothing to appear on TV and in the magazines. Generalizing broadly, they belong to one of two kinds: those who are working and those who aren't. Those who are working might go to a leper colony in India to promote their new record or TV show. The others can't afford to fly to India, but they might visit an orphanage in Tangiers or a prison in Rabat to keep themselves visible and boost their chances of getting some work soon. Not that either kind of personality necessarily goes to India or Morocco—those are just examples I'm using to make a general point: fame is measured in exclusives, calibrated by the size of the splash you can make with a scandal or a spectacular act of charity. But there was no such design behind my decision to foster a child for the month of July. No one knew anything about it, I mean no one who works for the glossy magazines. Olga's stay at my apartment was a secret, and during the days we spent on Mallorca with my family we kept well out of the public eye. I play the bimbo sometimes, if it's in the script, but I went to college and I earned my degree in art history.

So let me make it perfectly clear that I didn't want the girl for self-promotion. I have nothing against publicity as such, but there's a line between vulgar and sophisticated publicity. And that line should never be crossed, or so I was taught as a child, because there's no going back.

The next day I got a call from the NGO. They said they'd done everything humanly possible, but it wasn't going to be Olga. Instead they talked to me about Mariam, or María, a twelve-year-old Saharan girl who had lost her father in the war, a lovely girl, they said, and very clever for her age. Olga was twelve as well, I thought, and then I remembered her birthday and realized that I hadn't even sent her a card, and before I knew it I was crying, while the guy from the NGO went on giving me information about Mariam; she'd seen all sorts of atrocities, he said, and yet had somehow preserved her innocence. What do you mean? I asked. That's she's still a girl, in spite of everything she's been through. But she's twelve, I said. You haven't seen what I've seen, Lucía, he said in a velvety voice. The guy was trying to hit on me! He started telling me stories, not about the children, but about things that had happened to him. You have to travel a lot in this job. I travel a lot too, I said. I know, he said. For a while we talked about our respective travels. Then I agreed to foster Mariam and we said good-bye and hung up.

The only people I told were my parents and my sister. I didn't say anything to Gorka. Partly because he wasn't in Madrid (he'd gone to Mallorca for a sailing regatta), partly because I'm an independent woman and it was my decision and mine alone. Naturally, Gorka had plans for the summer, vague plans to go to an island in the Caribbean, and then to find a place in Mallorca, near his sailing friends, where we could stay till the beginning of September. I adore the sea. And I enjoy the regattas. I'm actually a better sailor than Gorka, who took it up quite recently (I've been sailing since I was a child), but like the rest of us, he's entitled to waste his time however he sees fit.

DEATH OF ULISES

Belano, our dear Arturo Belano, returns to Mexico City. More than twenty years have passed since the last time he was there. The plane is flying over the city, and he wakes with a start. The uneasiness he has felt throughout the trip intensifies. At the airport in Mexico City he has to catch a connecting flight to Guadalajara, for the Book Fair, to which he's been invited. Belano is now a fairly well-known author and is often invited to international events, although he doesn't travel much. This is his first trip to Mexico in more than twenty years. Last year he had two invitations and he pulled out at the last minute. The year before last he had four and he pulled out at the last minute. I can't remember how many invitations he had three years ago, but he pulled out at the last minute. Still, here he is in Mexico, in the Mexico City airport, following a group of perfect strangers who are heading toward the transit zone to catch the plane to Guadalajara. The corridor leads through a labyrinth of glass. Belano is the last in line. His steps are increasingly slow and hesitant. In a waiting room he spots a young Argentine writer who is also going to Guadalajara. Belano immediately takes cover behind a pillar. The Argentine is reading the paper, whose cultural supplement—maybe that's what he's reading—is entirely devoted to the Book Fair. After a few moments, he looks up and glances around, as if he knew he was being observed, but he doesn't see Belano, and his gaze returns to the paper. After a while a very beautiful woman approaches the Argentine and kisses him from behind. Belano knows her. She's a Mexican, born in Guadalajara. The Argentine man and the Mexican woman both live in Barcelona, together, and Belano is a friend of theirs. The Mexican woman and the Argentine man exchange a few words. Somehow both of them have sensed that they are being watched. Belano tries to read their lips, but he can't work out what they're saying. He doesn't leave his hiding place until their backs are turned. By the time he can finally escape from that corridor, the line of passengers heading for the connecting flight to Guadalajara has disappeared, and Belano realizes, with a deepening sense of relief, that he has no desire to go to Guadalajara and take part in the Book Fair; what he wants to do is to stay in Mexico City. And that is what he does. He heads for the exit. His passport is examined, and soon he's outside, looking for a taxi.

Back in Mexico, he thinks.

The taxi driver looks at him as if he were an old acquaintance. Belano has heard stories about the taxi drivers of Mexico City and muggings in the vicinity of the airport. But all those stories vanish now. Where are we going, young man? asks the driver, who is younger than Belano. Belano gives him the most recent address that he has for Ulises Lima. OK, says the driver, and the taxi pulls away and plunges into the city. Belano shuts his eyes, the way he used to when he lived there, but now he's so tired that he opens them almost immediately, and his old city, the city of his adolescence, displays itself to him for free. Nothing has changed, he thinks, although he knows that everything has changed.

It's a cemetery morning. The sky's a dirty yellow. The clouds, moving slowly from south to north, look like grave-yards adrift; sometimes they part to reveal scraps of gray sky, sometimes they come together with a dry, earthy grinding that no one, not even Belano, can hear, but it gives him a headache, the way it did when he was an adolescent and lived in Colonia Lindavista or Colonia Guadalupe-Tepeyac.

The people walking on the sidewalks, however, are the same; they're younger, they probably hadn't even been born when he left, but basically these are the faces he saw in 1968, in 1974, in 1976. The taxi driver tries to engage him in conversation, but Belano doesn't feel like talking. When he can finally close his eyes again, he sees his taxi driving at full speed down a busy avenue, while robbers hold up other taxis and the passengers die with terrified expressions on their faces. Vaguely familiar gestures and words. Fear. Then he sees nothing and falls asleep the way a stone falls down a well.

Here we are, says the taxi driver.

Belano looks out of the window. They're in the street where Ulises Lima used to live. He pays and gets out. Is this your first time in Mexico? asks the driver. No, I used to live here. Are you Mexican? the driver asks as he gives him the change. More or less, says Belano.

Then he's standing alone on the sidewalk, looking at the façade of the building.

Belano's hair is short. A bald patch like a tonsure reveals the top of his scalp. He's no longer the long-haired youth who once roamed these streets. Now he's wearing a black leather jacket and gray trousers and a white shirt and a pair of Martinelli shoes. He's been invited to Mexico to participate in a conference that will gather a group of Latin American writers. At least two of his friends have also been invited. His books are read (a bit) in Spain and Latin America, and all of them have been translated into various languages. What am I doing here? he wonders.

He walks toward the entrance of the building. He takes out his address book. He presses the buzzer of the apartment where Ulises Lima used to live. Three long buzzes. No one answers. He buzzes another apartment. A woman's voice asks who it is. I'm a friend of Ulises Lima, says Belano. She hangs up abruptly. He buzzes another apartment. A man's voice shouts, Who is it? A friend of Ulises Lima, says Belano, feeling more and more ridiculous. The door opens with an electric click, and Belano starts climbing the stairs to the third floor. By the time he reaches the landing, the effort is making him sweat. There are three doors and a long, dimly lit corridor. This is where Ulises Lima spent the last days of his life, he thinks, but when he rings the doorbell he finds himself irrationally hoping to hear his friend's approaching steps and then to see his smiling face appear at the crack in the door.

Nobody answers.

Belano goes back down the stairs. He finds a hotel nearby, without having to leave Colonia Cuauhtémoc. He sits on the bed for a long time, watching Mexican television and letting his mind go blank. Not a single show is familiar, but somehow the old shows infiltrate the new ones, and Belano has the impression that he can see the face of El Loco Valdés on the screen or hear his voice. Later, channel surfing, he comes across a Tin-Tan movie and watches to the end. Tin-Tan was El Loco's elder brother. He was already dead when Belano came to live in Mexico. El Loco Valdés might be dead now too.

When the movie's over, Belano takes a shower and then,

without even drying himself, he calls a friend. No one's home. Just the answering machine, but Belano doesn't want to leave a message.

He hangs up. He gets dressed. He goes to the window and looks out at Calle Río Panuco. He doesn't see people or cars or trees, only the gray pavement and a calm that has something timeless about it. Then a boy appears, walking down the opposite sidewalk with a young woman who might be his big sister or his mother. Belano shuts his eyes.

He isn't hungry, he isn't sleepy, he doesn't feel like going out. So he sits down on the bed again and goes on watching television, smoking one cigarette after another, until he finishes the pack. Then he puts on his black leather jacket and goes out into the street.

Irresistibly, the way a hit song keeps playing in your head, he finds himself returning to Ulises Lima's apartment.

The sun is beginning to set over Mexico City when, after a series of fruitless attempts, Belano succeeds in getting someone in the building to buzz him through the street door. I must be going crazy, he thinks, as he climbs the stairs two by two. Nothing's affecting me: the altitude, not having eaten, being alone in Mexico City. For a few interminable and, in their way, happy seconds, he stands in front of Ulises's door without ringing. Then he presses the button three times. As he is turning to go, about to leave the building (though not for the last time, he knows that), the door of the adjacent apartment opens and an enormous, hairless, coppery head, on which slashes of red can be dimly made out (as if the possessor of the head had been painting a wall or a ceiling), emerges and asks him who he's looking for.

At first, Belano doesn't know what to say. There's no point saying he's looking for Ulises Lima, and he can't be bothered making something up, so he keeps quiet and looks at his interlocutor: the head belongs to a young man, he wouldn't be more than twenty-five, and from his expression Belano guesses that he's annoyed or lives in a permanent state of annoyance. It's empty, that place, says the young man. I know, says Belano. So what are you ringing for, idiot? says the young man. Belano looks him in the eye and says nothing. The door opens and the hairless young man comes out into the corridor. He's fat, and all he's wearing is a pair of baggy jeans held up by an old belt. The buckle, partly hidden by the young man's belly, is large and made of metal. Is he coming out to hit me? wonders Belano. For a moment they examine each other. Our hero Arturo Belano, dear readers, is forty-six by this stage, and as you all know, or should know, his liver, his pancreas and even his colon are in a bad way, but he still knows how to box, and he's sizing up the voluminous figure in front of him. When he lived in Mexico he got into plenty of fights and never lost, though it's hard to credit now. Schoolyard scraps and barroom brawls. Belano looks at the fat guy, trying to figure out when to attack, when to hit him and where. But the fat guy just stares at Belano and looks back into his apartment, and then another young man appears, wearing a brown sweatshirt with a transfer on it that shows three men striking defiant poses in the middle of a street full of trash, and "Los Amos del Barrio" written in red letters at the top.

Belano is momentarily hypnotized by the design. Those pathetic-looking guys on the sweatshirt seem familiar. Or maybe not. Maybe it's the street that seems familiar. I've been there, years ago, he thinks, years ago I walked down that street, with time on my hands, just looking around.

The guy in the sweatshirt, who's almost as fat as the other one, asks Belano something in a voice that sounds like water boiling. Belano doesn't understand. But it wasn't an aggressive question, he's sure of that. What? he asks. Are you a fan of Los Amos del Barrio? repeats the fat guy in the sweatshirt.

Belano smiles. No, I'm not from here, he says.

Then the second fat guy is pushed aside and a third fat guy appears; he's very dark, an Aztec kind of fat guy with a little moustache, and he asks his roommates what's going on. Three against one, thinks Belano, time to go. The fat guy with the little moustache looks at him and asks what he wants. This jerk was ringing the bell at Ulises Lima's place, says the first fat guy. Did you know Ulises Lima? asks the fat guy with the little moustache. Yes, says Belano, I was a friend of his. And what's your name, jerk? asks the fat guy in the sweatshirt. Arturo Belano says his name and then adds that he'll be on his way, he's sorry to have bothered them, but now the three fat guys are looking at him with real interest, as if they were seeing him from a different point of view, and the fat guy in the sweatshirt smiles and says, Cut the bullshit, your name can't be Arturo Belano, though from the way he says it, Belano can tell that although he's unconvinced, he'd like to believe it's true.

Then he sees himself—and it's as if he's watching a movie, a movie so sad he'd never go to see it—in the fat guys' apartment, and they're offering their guest a beer. No thanks, I don't drink any more, he says, sitting in a rickety armchair, its cloth cover printed with wilting flowers, holding a glass of water he can't bring himself to drink from, because the water in Mexico City, so he's been warned, though in fact he's always known this, can give you gastroenteritis, while the fat guys settle down in the surrounding armchairs, except for the one without a shirt, who sits on the floor, as if he's afraid the other chair might break under his weight or afraid of how his friends might react if it did.

The fat guy without a shirt is behaving a bit like a slave, Belano thinks.

What happens next is chaotic and sentimental: the fat guys inform him that they were the last disciples of Ulises Lima (that's the word they use: *disciples*). They tell Belano about his death, how he was run down by a mysterious car, a black Impala, and they talk about his life, a succession of legendary drinking bouts, as if the bars and rooms where Ulises Lima got sick and threw up were the successive volumes of his complete works. But mainly they talk about themselves: they have a rock group called El Ojete de Morelos and they perform in discos in the suburbs of Mexico City. They've made a record, which the official radio stations won't touch because of the lyrics. But the little stations play their songs all day long. We're getting famous, they say, but we're still rebels. The way of Ulises Lima, they say, Ulises Lima's tracer fire, the poetry of Mexico's greatest poet.

As good as their word, they put on a CD of their songs, and Belano sits there motionless, listening, with his hand clamped around the glass of water he still hasn't sipped from, looking at the dirty floor and the walls covered with posters for Los Amos del Barrio and El Ojete de Morelos and other bands he's never heard of, maybe they're earlier groups, whose members went on to form Los Amos and El Ojete: Mexican kids staring out at him from photos or from hell, holding their electric guitars as if they were brandishing weapons or freezing to death.

THE TROUBLEMAKER

Some of his works were shown in 2003, during the European protests against the war in Iraq, at an exhibition organized by the poet Ponç Altés: mere sketches, as the artist pointed out himself, trials, private exercises done in some anonymous and dingy room. About Vallirana, there is little to be said: he was young, just twenty-one, unemployed, and he came from a family that was relatively poor (but loving: they supported him). His literary tastes were still developing, although he had, by then, read the complete works of Alfred Jarry, his favorite writer, whose radiance the passing days could do nothing to dim. As to Vallirana's personality at that time, the accounts diverge. Generally speaking, it could be said that he was a somewhat (though not excessively) reserved young man and somewhat shy (although his shyness was not excessive either). He believed only in art and science. For him, the union of art and science was a matter of *work*. In that sense it could be

said that he was deeply Catalonian. God and chance belonged
to art, eternity and labyrinths to science. When the protests
against the war in Iraq began, he spent three days shut up in
his room, like those young men in Japan who retreat to a tiny
bedroom in the family home and refuse to come out again to
look for work or go shopping or see a movie or take a walk in
the park. Being an only child and living in El Masnou, not
Tokyo, Vallirana had a larger bedroom, and he spent only
three days in there, watching television almost nonstop (there
was a set at the foot of his bed), barely sleeping, following the
protests, and thinking. When the three days were over, he
went up onto the roof and made a little sign. The sign said:
"NO WAR—LONG LIVE SADDAM HUSSEIN." He
wrote it in Roman square capitals—the result was rather styl-
ish—on a modest-sized sheet of white cardboard, which he
stapled onto a wooden stick about four feet long. In a moment
of malicious inspiration, he illustrated both sides of the sign
with little flowers that looked more like four-leafed clovers.
The next day he took the train to Barcelona and participated
in an anti-war demonstration in Hospitalet, which was poorly
attended, but that night he joined the crowd banging pots and
pans in Plaza San Jaume, and held his sign up high. No one
said anything to him in Hospitalet. Or in Plaza San Jaume,
where Vallirana contributed powerfully to the racket with an
umpire's whistle. He missed the last train back to El Masnou
and slept on a bench in the subway along with the homeless.
The next day he took part in a march with students from the
Universidad Autónoma, who chanted antiwar and anti-US
slogans as they walked from the campus to Sarrià, stopping the
traffic on numerous occasions. A girl who was studying jour-
nalism came up to him as they crossed one of the ring roads
and said that she was against the war but that didn't mean she
supported Saddam Hussein. The girl was called Dolors, and

Vallirana told her that his name was Enric de Montherlant. When the demonstration was over, they went to have coffee on Plaza de Sarrià, and agreed to meet the following day and join the big march from the Rambla de Catalunya to Plaza Catalunya. Then Vallirana went back to El Masnou, where he took a shower and changed his clothes, vaguely suspecting that he had picked up fleas the previous night. His whole body was, as it turned out, covered with tiny, bright red bites. Before going to sleep, Vallirana made a great many notes. He asked himself questions. And he didn't choose the lazy solution of leaving them all unanswered. When he'd finished writing, he went up to the rooftop terrace and made another sign. This one said: "NO WAR—LONG LIVE THE IRAQI PEOPLE—DEATH TO THE JEWS." The first phrase, NO WAR, was written in big letters, the second in smaller ones, and the third in letters that were smaller again. The characters had curves and twists that were vaguely reminiscent of Arabic script. Comic-book Arabic script. On both sides of the sign he drew peace symbols. When he had finished he said to himself: Now let's see what happens. Then he dined on a ham sandwich and tomato bread, and shut himself in his room and masturbated, thinking about Dolors, until he fell asleep, the TV on with the volume turned down so as not to bother his parents. First thing the next morning he caught a train. In his carriage there were laborers and students, but mainly commuters on the way to the office, men wearing ties and women in respectable, ugly suits, although, here and there, he could see a few people dressed with a little more taste, who didn't seem completely resigned to leading failed lives. These individuals seemed to have staked everything on sex and seduction, on attracting and being attracted, which wasn't much, thought Vallirana, but at least it was something. The others made a pitiful showing: women with glasses and too much fat on their hips and thighs, men who could only inspire disgust if they stripped off in a bedroom. As for the laborers, who were easily identifiable by their blue or yellow overalls and their lunch boxes or foil-wrapped sandwiches, they seemed to be in another world; and to a large extent they were, since most of them were immigrants from Africa or South America, who didn't care what the Spanish were doing. The students were dozing or going over their notes. When the train went into the tunnel in Barcelona, before reaching the Arco del Triunfo station, Vallirana shouted, "No war!" Some of the passengers, it seemed, were woken by the shout, and others were scared, but after the initial moment of surprise, almost everyone in the carriage responded by taking up the cry: "No war!"

SEVILLA KILLS ME

1. *The title.* In theory, and with no input from me whatsoever, the title of my talk was supposed to be "Where does the new Latin American novel come from?" If I stay on topic, my answer will be about three minutes long. We come from the middle classes or from a more or less settled proletariat or from families of low-level drug traffickers who're tired of gunshots and want respectability instead. As Pere Gimferrer says: in the old days, writers came from the upper classes or the aristocracy, and by choosing literature they chose—at least for a certain period that might be a lifetime or four or five years— social censure, the destruction of learned values, mockery and constant criticism. Now, on the other hand, especially in Latin America, writers come from the lower middle classes or from the ranks of the proletariat and what they want, at the end of the day, is a light veneer of respectability. That is, writers today seek recognition, though not the recognition of their

peers but of what are often called "political authorities," the usurpers of power, whatever century it is (the young writers don't care!), and thereby the recognition of the public, or book sales, which makes publishers happy but makes writers even happier, because these are writers who, as children at home, saw how hard it is to work eight hours a day, or nine or ten, which was how long their parents worked, and this was when there was work, because the only thing worse than working ten hours a day is not being able to work at all and having to drag oneself around looking for a job (paid, of course) in the labyrinth, or worse, in the hideous crossword puzzle of Latin America. So young writers have been burned, as they say, and they devote themselves body and soul to selling. Some rely more on their bodies, others on their souls, but in the end it's all about selling. What doesn't sell? Ah, that's an important consideration. Disruption doesn't sell. Writing that plumbs the depths with open eyes doesn't sell. For example: Macedonio Fernández doesn't sell. Macedonio may have been one of Borges's three great teachers (and Borges is or should be at the center of our canon) but never mind that. Everything says that we should read him, but Macedonio doesn't sell, so forget him. If Lamborghini doesn't sell, so much for Lamborghini. Wilcock is only known in Argentina and only by a few lucky readers. Forget Wilcock, then. Where does the new Latin American literature come from? The answer is very simple. It comes from fear. It comes from the terrible (and in a certain way fairly understandable) fear of working in an office and selling cheap trash on the Paseo Ahumada. It comes from the desire for respectability, which is simply a cover for fear. To those who don't know any better, we might seem like extras from a New York gangster movie, always talking about respect. Frankly, at first glance we're a pitiful group of writers in our thirties and forties, along with the occasional fifty-year-old, waiting for Godot, which in this case is the Nobel, the Rulfo, the Cervantes, the Príncipe de Asturias, the Rómulo Gallegos.

2. *The lecture must go on.* I hope no one takes what I just said the wrong way. I was kidding. I didn't mean what I wrote, or what I said. At this stage in my life I don't want to make any more unnecessary enemies. I'm here because I want to teach you to be men. Not true. Just kidding. Actually, it makes me insanely envious to look at you. Not just you but all young Latin American writers. You have a future, I promise you. Sorry. Kidding again. Your future is as a gray as the dictatorship of Castro, of Stroessner, of Pinochet, as the countless corrupt governments that follow one after the other on our continent. I hope no one tries to challenge me to a fight. I can't fight without medical authorization. In fact, when this talk is over I plan to lock myself in my room to watch pornography. You want me to visit the Cartuja? Fuck that. You want me to go see some flamenco? Wrong again. The only thing I'll see is a rodeo, Mexican or Chilean or Argentine. And once I'm there, amid the smell of fresh horse shit and flowering Chile-bells, I'll fall asleep and dream.

3. *The lecture must plant its feet firmly on the ground.* That's right. Let's plant our feet firmly on the ground. Some of the writers here are people I call friends. From them I expect nothing but perfect consideration. The rest of you I don't know, but I've read some of you and heard excellent things about others. Of course, certain writers are missing, writers without whom there's no understanding this entelechy that we call new Latin American literature. It's only fair to list them. I'll begin with the most difficult, a radical writer if there ever was one: Daniel Sada. And then I should mention César Aira, Juan Villoro, Alan Pauls, Rodrigo Rey Rosa, Ibsen Martínez, Carmen

Boullosa, the very young Antonio Ungar, the Chileans Gonzalo Contreras, Pedro Lemebel, Jaime Collyer, Alberto Fuguet, and María Moreno, and Mario Bellatin, who has the fortune or misfortune of being considered Mexican by the Mexicans and Peruvian by the Peruvians, and I could go on like this for at least another minute. It's a promising scene, especially if viewed from a bridge. The river is wide and mighty and its surface is broken by the heads of at least twenty-five writers under fifty, under forty, under thirty. How many will drown? I'd say all of them.

4. *The inheritance.* The treasure left to us by our parents, or by those we thought were our putative parents, is pitiful. In fact, we're like children trapped in the mansion of a pedophile. Some of you will say that it's better to be at the mercy of a pedophile than a killer. You're right. But our pedophiles are also killers.

NATASHA WIMMER

THE DAYS OF CHAOS

Just when Arturo Belano thought that all his adventures were over and done with, his wife, the woman who had been his wife and still was and probably would be until the end of his days (legally speaking, at least), came to see him in his apartment by the sea and announced that their son, the handsome young Gerónimo, had disappeared in Berlin during the Days of Chaos.

This was in the year 2005.

Arturo packed his bags and that night he boarded a plane bound for Berlin. He arrived at three in the morning. From the window of the taxi he observed that the city was at least outwardly calm, although he glimpsed the vehicles of the riot police and fires burning here and there in the streets. But in general everything seemed calm; the city was under sedation.

This was in the year 2005.

Arturo Belano was over fifty and Gerónimo was fifteen.

Géronimo had gone to Berlin with a group of friends; it was the first time he'd traveled without one of his parents. The morning Arturo's wife came over, the group had just returned, minus Gerónimo and another boy called Félix, whom Arturo remembered as very tall and thin and pimply. Arturo had known Félix since the kid was five years old. Sometimes, when he went to pick up his son from school, Félix and Gerónimo would stay and play in the park for a while. In fact, they might even have met one another for the first time in preschool, before either of them was three, though Arturo couldn't remember having seen Félix's face back then. Félix wasn't his son's best friend, but there was a kind of familiarity between them.

This was in the year 2005.

Gerónimo Belano was fifteen. Arturo Belano was over fifty, and sometimes he could barely believe that he was still alive. Arturo had set off on his first long trip at the age of fifteen too. His parents had decided to leave Chile and start a new life in Mexico.